W9-AAZ-815

Casa
Azul

Casa Azul

An Encounter with Frida Kahlo

LABAN CARRICK HILL

WATSON-GUPTILL PUBLICATIONS/NEW YORK

Senior Editor: Jacqueline Ching
Editor: Laaren Brown
Production Manager: Hector Campbell
Book Design: Jennifer Browne

First published in 2005 in the United States by Watson-Guptill Publications,
a division of VNU Business Media, Inc.,
770 Broadway, New York, NY 10003
www.wgpub.com

Front cover: Frida Kahlo, *Self-Portrait with Thorn Necklace and Hummingbird,* c. 1940. Art Collection,
Harry Ransom Humanities Research Center, The University of Texas at Austin.
Excerpt on p. 92 from *The Diary of Frida Kahlo: An Intimate Self-Portrait.* Introduction by Carlos Fuentes;
essay and commentaries by Sarah M. Lowe (New York: Harry N. Abrams, 2001), pp. 231-2
Chapter art from *Design Motifs of Ancient Mexico* by Jorge Enciso, Dover Publications, Inc., copyright 1947.

Library of Congress Cataloging-in-Publication Data
Hill, Laban Carrick.
Casa Azul / by Laban Carrick Hill.
p. cm.
Summary: In 1940, after traveling from their country village to Mexico City to find their mother,
fourteen-year-old Maria and her younger brother Victor are befriended by the artist Frida Kahlo
and the talking animals and household objects that inhabit her home.
Includes bibliographical references and index.
ISBN 0-8230-0411-2 (alk. paper)
1. Kahlo, Frida—Juvenile fiction. [1. Kahlo, Frida—Fiction. 2. Brothers and sisters—Fiction.
3. Mexico City (Mexico)—History—20th century—Fiction. 4. Animals—Fiction. 5. Artists—Fiction.
6. Rivera, Diego, 1886-1957—Fiction. 7. Mexico—History—1910-1946—Fiction.] I. Title.
PZ7.H55286Cas 2005
[Fic]—dc22
2004023300

This book was set in Stempel Garamond.

Printed in the U.S.A.
First printing, 2005
1 2 3 4 5 6 7 8 9 / 12 11 10 09 08 07 06 05

For Susan Pfau,
my big sister,
who always knew what was best for me,
whether I agreed or not

Contents

Preface   ix

1   A Journey   1

2   The Saddest Day in the World   8

3   The Great Heart of Mexico   13

4   Casa Azul   20

5   Old Big Eyes   30

6   Advice from Dr. Eloesser   36

7   A Magic Trick   41

8   Backstreets   46

9   Dinner and a Story   51

10   No Hope at All   58

11   A Thief's Life   66

12   Wrestle Mania   72

13   A Good Deed   76

14   Cold Alley   80

15   Painting the World   86

16   Lourdes 27   92

17   *Retablo*   100

18   A Magical World   106

19   Hope   116

20   Help from Diego   122

21   Monkey Shines   127

22   A New Happiness   133

23   A New Portrait   135

Frida Kahlo's Life and Art   138

A Timeline of Kahlo's Life   144

For More Information   148

Preface

Casa *Azul* is full of lies. All novels are full of lies. The irony is that it takes lies to tell the Truth. That is, the Truth with a capital *T*, not the truth about whether you ate the last chocolate chip cookie or not. Stories allow us to discover something essential about ourselves and about the human condition. The reason stories work so well is because they are not limited by the facts of real life. The problem with real life is that it does not always add up. So much seems random and pointless, in a word, accidental. Stories bend and change facts in order to reveal the Truth, which real life can never really successfully do.

Casa Azul combines some of the facts about Frida Kahlo's life with some outright lies to uncover the essence of her motivation to create. Kahlo herself was an aficionado of lying. After she became a communist, she changed the date of her birth from 1907 to 1910 to reflect her solidarity with the start of the Mexican Revolution. As an artist, she created a world on canvas that stepped beyond simply representing what she saw with her eyes. "I paint my own reality," she once said. "The only thing I know is that I paint because I need to, and I paint whatever passes through my head, without any other consideration." As a result, her paintings included images of things that could never exist in the real world.

In her painting *Self-Portrait with Thorn Necklace and Hummingbird*, she tried to reveal to the viewer the kind of tension between suffering and beauty that she lived with every day. The painting depicts her as regal and accepting, while the monkey and cat on her shoulders are caught somewhere between menace and peace. The painting is ambiguous because Kahlo felt that life never presented clear choices. The painting is strange, and very unreal. No one would wear a thorn necklace with a dead hummingbird hanging from it as a pendant. There are flowers with wings like butterflies hovering over her head. The tropical leaves in the background seem pressed against glass, eliminating depth and perspective. The world depicted in this painting is wholly constructed. It could never exist outside the painting.

This kind of art was called surrealism. *Sur* is a prefix that means "beyond" or "over," so *surrealism* means "beyond realism." Kahlo's paintings used surrealism to articulate her emotional reality, which did not always align with the facts of her life.

This novel attempts to do the same not only with Kahlo's life, but also with the lives of Maria and Victor Ortiz. Set in 1940, the year the famous artist Diego Rivera divorced Kahlo, *Casa Azul* brings the reader into a fantasy world that is based in reality but that also steps beyond the rules of normal everyday life. This is the story of two children who encounter Frida Kahlo under extraordinary circumstances. Like Kahlo's paintings, the story you are about to read is truly unbelievable because it is meant to tell you something you can believe.

CHAPTER ONE

A Journey

"No, Father," answered Maria Ortiz. Her eyes were cast downward at the ground because she was embarrassed about disobeying her priest. She played nervously with the beautiful turquoise brooch pinned to her blouse. The silver in the brooch caught the morning light and reflected in her eyes.

"Please, there are good families here who will take you in—you and your brother," pressed Father Michelangelo. His pale face tensed under the wisp of a beard that covered his jaw. He placed his hand on Victor's shoulder and glanced down the dirt track lined with adobe buildings on each side. Beyond, fields of corn and grain spread out along a creek that flowed through the town.

Maria glared at Father Michelangelo, then guiltily locked her eyes again on the ground and shook her head firmly. Her hair tumbled over her face, so the priest could not see it. She touched the brooch again as if it were some kind of talisman from which she could draw courage. She did not like going against the priest's wishes, but she was the head of her family now. It was her decision to make. "Father . . . I'm old enough to marry and have children. I can take care of my brother."

"I want to go with Maria," Victor said as he gripped his older sister's hand.

The three stood silently under the hot Mexican sun. The air around them radiated with heat, creating mirages of shimmering puddles in the distance. At Maria's feet was a small, battered cardboard suitcase held together with a knotted piece of twine. It contained all of Maria and Victor's belongings—a change of clothes, a photograph of their mother, and food for the trip.

"Victor is just a boy," pleaded Father Michelangelo. "At least leave him with me. I could take care of him until you find your mother."

"It's not your decision," answered Maria firmly. She was fourteen years old now, and had long been caring for her brother, who was six years younger.

She looked at the priest defiantly and saw the ropes of sweat streaming down his face and plastering his short-cropped hair to his head. Anyone who wore heavy black wool robes in this heat did not have the sense to take care of children. She felt cool in comparison, dressed in her best traditional Tehuana costume with the elaborate blue ribbons her grandmother had sewn on it. Earlier that morning she had pressed its stiff, colorful cotton fabric with an iron heated on the wood stove.

Victor pulled on his sister's hand. "When will the bus come?" She sighed. Victor had started acting even younger than he was.

"Soon, *poquito*." Maria glanced down the dirt track for any sign of the bus. "When we get to Mexico City, I'll buy you a toy."

"Really? Promise?" Barely up to her shoulders, the boy wore the worn canvas pants, coarse shirt, and straw sombrero of a peasant, and like his sister, on his feet were handmade sandals.

"*Sí*, I promise." Maria squeezed her brother's hand tightly to reassure him that she would never leave him. "Now, go play."

Time passed slowly while Maria stared impatiently down the dry, dusty road at a stand of banyan trees. She was so tired of this boring village. She desperately wanted to see the city—where everything was happening. There was nothing left for her or her brother here. She watched the leaves rustle gently in a slight breeze.

"You don't have to wait with us," she told the priest, trying to hint that she'd like to be left alone.

"I can't leave you now," he protested, indignant at the suggestion.

Maria gritted her teeth. Father Michelangelo meant well, even if he didn't understand. She wished she could leave him and wait for the bus in the shade of those trees. But that would be disrespectful to the priest, who was the most important person in her village.

Instead, she stayed in the harsh sunlight in front of the small adobe church, La Asunción de Maria. Like the village, this was the only church she had ever known. The village of Xtogon was nothing more than a dozen one-room adobe houses, one of which served as the *bodega*. The church was the largest structure in town, and during the rainy season, it served as the school as well. The small cemetery beside the church held one new grave covered with freshly turned earth. A small, plain white cross stood at its head. Maria took pains not to look that way as she and her brother waited, and at the same time she stood between Victor and the cemetery so that he would not look either.

"Your grandmother would not have approved," Father Michelangelo said with finality.

"My grandmother is dead," replied Maria, as a deep sadness bloomed on her face. She fought to hold back the tears, but one escaped. She quickly wiped it away with a dusty hand, leaving a streak across her cheek. "And all I have left of her is this brooch." She fingered the jewelry once again.

"Don't lose it," replied the priest automatically.

I'm not a child, she thought bitterly. *Why can't he understand this?*

In the tense silence, she watched Victor as he chased a small lizard crawling up the wall of the church. His quick hand snatched at the scrambling creature, but he only captured the lizard's tail, which broke away easily. In a matter of days the lizard would grow a new one. Maria saw Victor pocket the tail and knew he would play with it on the long bus ride.

Just then dozens of bright green parrots exploded from the banyan trees down the road. Like a green blanket tossed across the sky, the parrots circled above and settled in a new tree farther from the road. Their caws drowned out the wheeze and rumble of an ancient bus, that suddenly came into sight. All three watched the battered vehicle sway toward them along the deeply rutted track. The driver honked twice to announce its arrival, and the bus lurched into the village. Grinding its brakes, it slowed to a stop in front of the church. The driver cranked open the door and looked at the three people. The windows on this bus had long ago been removed. Passengers hung out the openings along the side and stared at them. They were mostly peasants traveling from one village to the next in search of work or, if they had the fare, heading to Mexico City to start a new life.

"Wait," said Father Michelangelo. He hurried across the street. His robes dragged along the ground, sending up plumes of dust. He slipped into an adobe shack with smoke coming lazily out of its chimney. Maria and Victor stood there for a moment. They looked inside the bus and saw that it was full. Standing room only. The driver pointed to the luggage rack above. Maria and Victor could see the faces of passengers between the suitcases and cages holding chickens.

"It's much cooler up here," called down a man in a black suit and a torn straw hat.

"Really?" Maria nodded and dug into her purse for the money to pay the fares. She turned her back to the bus so no one could see exactly how much money she had. Once the driver had given her two tickets in exchange, a hand reached down from above. Maria grabbed it and allowed herself to be lifted onto the bus's roof. She thanked the man in the black suit. The driver stepped from the bus and hoisted Victor so he could be pulled up as well.

The driver closed the door and gunned the engine before putting the bus in gear.

"Wait!" called Father Michelangelo as he emerged from the shack. He was carrying a paper bag that was already soaked with grease. He handed up the bag to Maria. "Here are some tamales for your ride."

"Thank you, Father, for all that you have done," said Maria.

She and her brother were perched like birds atop the tied-down luggage. Next to them and the man in the black suit were two others,

a young couple not much older than Maria, who had wedged them-
selves between two wooden crates. They both bowed their heads
and smiled.

"Why don't you tell Victor one of your stories?" Father Michelangelo called up. He smiled and bounced nervously on the balls of his
feet, as if he were trying to rise to the height of the bus's roof so he
could confirm that Maria and Victor were safe. "Perhaps one about
his wrestlers. Victor loves them so."

Maria nodded. "I will, Father." She banged her fist on the roof to
signal the driver to leave.

"This trip will give you lots of adventures for your stories," the
priest added. "I'll see you when you return."

"Good-bye, Father," called Maria.

"Come back soon," called the priest. He raised his arm and
waved.

The driver shifted into gear and the bus rolled down the rutted
track toward the next village, as it would all the way to the capital,
Mexico City. Below, inside the bus, somebody began to play a guitar
and sing.

> "*Mira que si te quisé, fué por el pelo.*
> *Ahora que no lo tienes, ya no te quiero.*"

> "Look if I loved you, it was for your hair.
> Now that you are bald, I don't love you anymore."

Everyone on the bus laughed. The man next to the woman on

the roof whispered in her ear, "I would always love you even if you were bald."

The woman laughed and hit his shoulder. "If you were bald, I would drop you like a hot tamale."

Maria and Victor watched as the priest and his waving arm got smaller and smaller until both disappeared below the horizon.

"I thought we'd never go," muttered Maria. All she wanted to do was think about the adventures that lay ahead, and try to forget the painful memories that were left behind.

Maria stared out at the dry, spare landscape. On the thin spikes of a magueys plant by the rutted dirt road, a torn red bandanna fluttered in the breeze. It reminded her of the red cape the matador used to taunt the bull at the Day of the Dead festival.

CHAPTER TWO

The Saddest Day in the World

With bright red ribbons tumbling from her tightly braided hair, a crying woman stood unwillingly in a courtroom three hundred miles north, far from the green fields and adobe village of Maria and Victor's home. Her marriage to the man she still loved was about to be torn asunder.

Like all divorces, this was a formal affair, set in a courtroom before a judge. There were lawyers for both sides and spectators in the gallery. Reporters for all of Mexico City's newspapers were waiting as well, because this wasn't the end of just any marriage. This was the divorce of Frida Kahlo and Diego Rivera, two of Mexico's greatest living artists. They were so famous that they were always referred to by their first names.

For Mexico this was a sad day. But for Frida this was the saddest day in the world. She never imagined that her marriage to Diego would end. The newspapers called their marriage a "union of lions." Their love, their battles, their separations, and their sufferings were beyond the petty concerns of normal couples. Even at this moment when their marriage would be cast aside like a pair of old shoes, Frida believed deep in her heart that Diego belonged to her and she belonged to him.

"All rise! The Honorable Miguel Figuenza is presiding," called out the court reporter as he banged the gavel.

Everyone rose as the judge entered the courtroom from a door hidden behind the raised desk.

Nervously, Frida watched him, wiping her tears away.

She turned and thrust out her chin at Diego. "Look at him," Frida seemed to say to no one but the pet monkey on her shoulder. "He looks like he's enjoying himself. I could strangle him."

Diego stood on the opposite side of the courtroom with his hat in his hand and his head bowed. He looked anything but happy.

"He probably has that woman waiting for him outside the courthouse," she continued. "Now he can go cheat on some other woman."

The monkey seemed to be trying to comfort Frida by speaking to her, but it was only chatter. Perched on her shoulder, Fulang was dressed like Frida in traditional Tehuana costume. As a show of solidarity to the *campesinos*, Frida dressed herself, and sometimes her pets, in peasant clothes worn in the countryside: a starched white blouse decorated with ruffles, a full red velvet skirt embroidered with ribbons, a woven shawl called a *rebozo* draped across the shoulders, and a beaded jade necklace. Fulang delicately picked dried mango from Frida's hand and ate the sweet pieces. Her small fingers reminded Frida of a child's, the child she knew she would never have.

Just as quickly as her anger flared, Frida was overwhelmed with sadness and memories. "Diego courted me in a room very much like this one," Frida whispered hoarsely. Fulang nodded as if she understood. Frida glanced up at the huge mural covering the wall behind the judge. "Twelve years ago I brought three paintings for him to see while he was painting a mural in the Ministry of Public Education."

Fulang cooed, again as if she understood.

Frida lost herself in the memory of seeing Diego standing like a giant on the tall scaffolding, painting the image of *campesinos*, Mexico's peasants, rising up against the brutal land owners. "His paintings were the most beautiful I had ever seen. They showed the people with all their hopes and aspirations marching toward a more perfect world. His browns were the color of the people, and his strokes with his paintbrush made the crops come alive."

She smiled as she remembered Diego in his green overalls and wide-brimmed hat, announcing, "Art is like ham. It nourishes people." She had written the words in her diary, along with everything else from that time. And she had returned to these pages time and again over the years and memorized the passages. Now she recalled them as the proceedings around her receded from her consciousness and happy memories took over.

"Meeting Diego was the first good thing that happened to me after the accident," Frida said.

Fulang dipped her head just like someone who was listening.

"I've told you about the accident before. How I was almost killed when a trolley struck the bus I was riding in. But that's not what I want to talk about now." Frida paused and lost herself in the memory. "Diego was like a giant knight in shining armor bringing light to the people."

The court proceedings began, but Frida was oblivious to them now.

"The first moment I was allowed to walk, I went immediately to see Diego. I had been painting since the accident and knew that only he could tell me if my paintings were worth anything. When I got to the ministry, I called to him. 'Diego, come down here now.' He laughed at my boldness, but he came down. And I told him I was here not to flirt but for art. He looked at my paintings and told me to paint some more. Then he said: 'You have talent.'"

Though her actions seemed naive to her now, Frida knew that they were true. She had been only eighteen, and had just recovered from a bus accident in which the handrail of the trolley had driven through her body. This tragedy had given her an understanding of the world beyond her years. She then put that pain and suffering in her painting, and through this she had discovered a gift. She had been made sensitive to the world. Her life, like her art, could communicate in ways unknown to others.

"Is the petition before me agreed upon by both parties?" asked Judge Figuenza.

Frida was startled out of her reverie by the judge's words. She nodded and whispered, "Yes, Your Honor." She gazed at Diego as she repeated these words louder so that the entire court could hear. She still loved this giant frog of a man, but he had abandoned her for reasons Frida could not fathom.

As the judge finalized the divorce, Diego broke with decorum and crossed the courtroom. He held out his hands as if he was asking her to forgive him. Frida stood still as she watched him come, while Fulang hissed and bared her teeth.

"Frida," said Diego. "I love you, but you cannot waste yourself on me. Mexico deserves more. Your art deserves more." His massive shoulders slumped.

"Go back to your *cochinada*, your piggery," spat Frida. She took a painful step backward for she would never recover from the accident. Then suddenly a mean and tight smile spread across her face. She reached down and grabbed Diego's crotch. "You will be back soon enough . . . when you tire of your whores."

"Listen to me," pressed Diego. "This divorce must happen if you are going to step out of my shadow. I have watched it kill you, but more importantly, kill your painting. I will not be responsible any longer."

Just as quickly, Frida's emotions swung again and tears rolled down her cheeks. She felt confused by Diego's words. "But I cannot live without you!" she pleaded.

"You must," Diego said with finality. As he turned to leave, Frida gripped his sleeve and fell stiffly to her knees. Fulang tried to wipe the tears from Frida's cheeks.

Diego pulled himself free and disappeared into the corridor.

CHAPTER THREE

The Great Heart of Mexico

"I'm scared."

Maria snaked her arm around her little brother's small shoulders and pulled him close. Squeezed between chicken cages and crates on the roof of an ancient bus, she felt strong being able to comfort Victor. Together they rocked on top of the bus as it made its way down the uneven burro track that now served as the highway between their village and Mexico City.

"Everything will be fine," Maria cooed. She could feel that her brother's muscles were knotted and tense but so were hers. Still, she tried to keep her voice calm and comforting. "We're going to have so much fun in Mexico City. It'll be better than even the *biggest* fiesta in Xtogon."

"But what about Mama?" asked Victor. "I want to find her."

"Oh, we will. Once we get to Mexico City we'll find Mama and she'll take care of you." For Maria, the trip was just as much about being free of the small village and on her own, away from adults who treated her like a child, as it was about finding their mother.

"Do you know where your mother is?" asked the young woman across from Maria.

"*Sí*, I have the address where she works," explained Maria. "Last year she went to the city to work for a rich family."

"*Bueno*," said the young woman. "Mexico City is not a place to be lost in." Maria did not mention that she had not heard from her mother in weeks and that her father had left years before and disappeared too. In reality, she didn't want to admit to herself that her mother might be gone forever. Now that her grandmother had passed away, she was determined not to lose her mother the same way as her father.

Maria watched Victor pick at the small hole at the cuff of his shirt. "Stop that," she said with the same tone her mother used to use. "You'll ruin your only good shirt."

"Tell me about El Corazón," Victor whispered. He buried his head in his sister's shoulder. "I wish Grandma was here. She could find Mama."

As their grandmother had grown sicker, Father Michelangelo had written to their mother at the address she had left them. The letter was never answered. Maria tried not to think about this. She knew it must be a mistake.

"A story, please, Maricita," pleaded Victor. He squeezed her hand tightly.

Maria looked out across the dry, rocky landscape to gather her thoughts. She had been telling Victor wrestling stories for years. She began her latest tale. "As you know, El Corazón, the great heart of Mexico, beat El Perro, the dog, for the wrestling championship of the world."

"*Sí, sí*, and he hurt his shoulder early in the match and had to beat that dirty dog with only one arm," Victor added. Back in their village the entire town would gather each week in the plaza to hear Father Michelangelo read the newspaper's account of the Saturday night matches at the arena in Mexico City. Maria and Victor would beg their grandmother to buy the newest edition of *Wrestling Comics* when it arrived each month. They would pour over the pictures and imagine what it would be like to see these great warriors in real life. Maria would then make up stories about the wrestlers and the matches they fought to entertain her little brother.

"Can we go to the wrestling matches at the arena?" asked Victor, getting excited. Maria was glad to see him forget about his troubles as he thought about the possibility of seeing these great wrestlers in person.

"Of course." Maria laughed, knowing she really didn't mean it. "Now let me tell the story." She sat up straight against the chicken cages and thought for a moment. Then a smile spread across her face. "El Corazón's archenemy is El Diablo." Maria made the sign of the cross with her hand over her chest to protect herself from such evil. Victor mimicked his sister. "There is no wrestler more evil than he."

Victor nodded. "He is meaner than that rabid dog, El Perro." He made as if to spit but his sister put her hand on his shoulder to stop him. Only the lowliest animals on the earth spit, their mother always told them.

"*Sí.*" Maria paused dramatically. The other passengers on the roof of the bus had become interested in the story as well and were now listening intently. "This night at the Mexico City Arena, El Corazón is matched against that villain El Diablo."

Everyone on the roof of the bus made the sign of the cross.

"Oh, he's going to murder him," Victor said excitedly.

"Victor," Maria said sharply. "We don't wish that on anyone."

"Not even El Diablo?" he asked.

"Not even him. Father Michelangelo says it is okay to wish that a wrestler loses a match, but never death."

"Maybe a broken leg then?"

"No."

"Hand?"

"No."

Victor hung his head in disappointment.

"When El Corazón enters the arena, the crowd erupts in cheers," Maria described. "Women faint at the sight of him. Men leap to their feet and scream like little boys."

"Not me," Victor interrupted, puffing out his chest.

Maria got Victor in a headlock and rubbed her knuckle against his skull. "Yes, you!"

The other passengers laughed.

"Now, are you going to let me tell the story?"

Victor nodded.

"El Corazón was dressed in white satin tights that shimmered in the lights. His mask covered his entire head, and it had a bloodred heart over his face. His cape was white fur, as light as a feather. It also had a bloodred heart sewn in its center. When he climbed into the ring, he raised his arms and drank in the crowd's love. He blew kisses and bowed. It was clear that El Corazón loved his fans as much as they loved him. But before the cheers died . . ."

Maria paused and looked at her listeners. The couple smiled back at her, while the man in the black suit waved his hand to encourage her to continue.

"El Diablo dashed into the ring and leaped onto El Corazón's back."

"Oh no," murmured the man sitting next to his wife.

"*Sí*. The referee had not yet entered the ring, and that scoundrel had made a sneaky attack." Maria shrugged. "There was nothing else to do but start the match. The timekeeper rang the bell and the referee slid under the bottom rope, still tying his shoes.

"El Diablo had El Corazón in an illegal choke hold. His notorious and deadly Sleeper Hold. As you remember, no one has ever escaped from El Diablo's Sleeper Hold."

"No!" cried Victor.

"*Sí*," Maria said with finality. "The match was in danger of being over before it had even begun. The referee started his count to disqualify El Diablo, but then El Corazón took measures into his own hands. He backed up very fast and slammed the evil one into a turnbuckle. This stunned El Diablo, and El Corazón took advantage and delivered a forearm to the chest."

Victor clapped his hands together in delight

"Then he grabbed El Diablo's arm and swung him across the ring into the other turnbuckle," explained Maria. "With quick efficiency, he planted his foot in the devil's stomach. El Diablo bent over as if he were badly hurt. But he wasn't."

"Watch out!" shouted Victor.

Maria nodded. "He was just tricking El Corazón. So when El

Corazón approached to finish off this piece of garbage, El Diablo struck. He rammed his head into our hero's stomach. El Corazón staggered backward, and El Diablo delivered a flying kick, sending him into the ropes. When he bounced back, El Diablo wrapped his arms around El Corazón's chest and tossed him over his head like a sack of *masa harina*."

The passengers on the roof groaned.

"*Sí*. It was terrible. The match had hardly started and it looked as if El Corazón was finished. He lay writhing in pain on the canvas. El Diablo celebrated by waving his fists at the booing crowd. To add insult to injury, he leaped into the air and slammed his arm against El Corazón's chest. Then he pinned El Corazón to the mat. The referee dashed across the ring and began to count our hero out."

"No!" cried Victor.

"One!"

"Save yourself, El Corazón!"

"Two!"

"Get up!"

"But before the referee could slap his hand against the mat a third time, El Corazón kicked out, throwing the devil off him and lifting his shoulders."

The rooftop passengers cheered.

"It was close, but El Corazón summoned just enough strength from the love of his fans, because, as you know, that is where he gains his power to fight. The crowd went wild as El Corazón leaped to his feet and slapped his hand against his heart to indicate that his heart beat for them."

As she told the story, Maria watched her little brother. She was relieved to see that he had forgotten his worries, but she could not forget hers.

Memories of her grandmother's death filled her with sadness. In her mind's eye, she could see her grandmother wasting away with fever. Each day for the past month, Grandmother had became paler and thinner until she could almost blow away in a stiff wind. It was as if she had grown so slight that her body could no longer hold on to her soul. So two nights earlier, exhausted from all the worry and work she'd been doing, Maria had slept for the first time in days. And that was the night her grandmother's soul rose up to heaven. The next morning Maria discovered her dead. In her heart she believed that if she had been there and had not been sleeping she could have caught the soul and not allowed it to leave her grandmother. She would do a better job of protecting Victor.

CHAPTER FOUR

Casa Azul

Upon returning from the courthouse, Frida shooed Fulang away to play in the courtyard of Casa Azul, the childhood home to which she had returned. "Beat it, monkey!" she snapped harshly, using the American slang she loved so much.

Fulang leaped from her shoulder onto a low-hanging branch of a plane tree. She started to say something but thought better of it and disappeared into the upper branches. Now that they were back at Frida's house, Fulang could have spoken back.

Inside, Frida wandered aimlessly from room to room, absent-mindedly picking up belongings—a hairbrush, a candy Day of the Dead skull, a paintbrush—returning each to its place without really recognizing what she had just held. As she passed through her home, the paintings, the photographs, the sculptures—anything with a face—did not just seem to watch her, they actually did. Her home was alive in ways that other homes would never be.

Years before, a miracle had descended upon her life out of the ashes of pain and tragedy. Frida had been given the gift of making her home a haven for all things. Anything that crossed her threshold, whether it was living or inanimate, could speak, as long as it had a mouth. But this gift did not come easily. It was a gift from the spirits, who had taken pity on her after her terrible accident.

She had been just a teenager in 1925, riding home on a bus after shopping. The driver turned too slowly in front of an oncoming trolley. The collision crushed the bus and broke nearly every bone in Frida's body.

This accident seemed to tap into an ancient awareness, something pre-colonial, from the days of the Aztec empire. Aztecs believed in a shared consciousness among all beings. Through this power, people could communicate with things not human. After her accident, Frida discovered that for anyone who entered Casa Azul, this was not just legend; it was true. They could hear the voices of the world around them and could speak to them.

Now in Casa Azul, Frida drifted as if in a dream among her things until she came to her bedroom. There she collapsed on her bed, dazed by the events of the day. On the pillow in a square of warm sunlight lay Chica, her black cat.

Leaping up, Chica meowed. "Hey!"

"Beat it, rat trapper!"

Chica leaped off the bed. "Well, excuse me, Miss Moody." Then she padded across the room and settled in another patch of sunlight on the floor. Her black fur shimmered like velvet.

Frida turned away from her cat. "I don't need this abuse."

"*Qué?* What?" said Chica. *I was the one lying there innocently sunning herself when Frida had come in and started it,* she thought. *What is* her *problem?*

Frida was lost in her own thoughts and could not imagine what the rest of the day and the next and the day after that would be like alone—without Diego. She had married him twelve years before and moved from this house, Casa Azul, to Diego's studio. A few years earlier, he had built them a home with adjoining studios. Now that was gone.

As Frida's mind danced over the memories, her eyes stared up at the canopy above her bed. Because she had had to spend so much recovery time in bed, it was decorated with Day of the Dead skeletons, ribbons, and odds and ends that had caught her fancy over the years. A glass box was suspended just overhead. It was filled with dried butterflies. In the shadows of the canopy, the bright-colored wings seemed to glow. The intense blues, garish greens, pulsing oranges, and deep, rich reds held her attention, and disgusted her. "How can you be so bright and gay on a day like this?" she challenged the dead butterflies.

Trapped in their glass box, the butterflies responded with simply a muffled cry.

Clearly annoyed, Frida reached up and pulled the glass box free. Violently, she opened it and poured out the butterflies. Their cries whispered as they drifted toward the floor.

At this the candy Day of the Dead skull on the windowsill became alarmed. He knew Frida loved those butterflies and had placed them on her canopy so she could gaze at them always.

"Psssst!" he whispered, with the kind of awkward lisp a mouth with no lips would have. He did not want Frida to hear. "Psssst!"

Chica raised her head and saw what Frida had done. Quickly, she jumped to the windowsill. "Fulang!"

Outside the window, Fulang rested on a branch. She was watching one of the wild monkeys of the neighborhood fly through the trees chasing squirrels. He seemed so quick and strong. He was handsome, with a toothy smile that flashed at a moment's notice. Fulang had been admiring the monkey since he had moved into the neighborhood. She wanted to get his attention, but she was too shy to speak. Instead, she chewed at a flea on her shoulder as her eyes studied the remarkable monkey playing high in the branches nearby.

"Fulang!" Chica hopped onto the tree branch by the window and swiped at the monkey.

Startled, Fulang stumbled off the branch and fell to the ground. "Watch what you're doing!"

Chica motioned toward the window.

On the windowsill the skull made as if he had eyeballs and could roll them. Fulang leaped to the sill. Chica followed. Inside, Frida was untying the ribbons around her bed's canopy. When she was done, she took the ribbons out of her hair and off the hem of her skirt as well. It was as if she was removing all gaiety from the room.

Alarmed, Fulang hopped to the easel propped in a corner, where a portrait of Diego in large green overalls and an expansive cowboy hat sat nearly done. Fulang nudged the portrait. "Do something!" The portrait of Diego glanced up at Fulang, for it was alive too. Its eyes followed the monkey's gaze to where Frida was carefully wrapping a portrait of her sister with ribbons. It was as if she were covering the entire image in bandages, or cloaking it as the images in a church were covered on Holy Thursday.

"Frida!" the image of Diego commanded. "Stop that!"

Frida turned to her nearly finished painting of Diego and smiled. "You don't matter anymore. You toad!" She held up a handful of ribbons. "These are for you." She wrapped Diego's portrait.

"Stop this!" the portrait protested in a muffled voice. "You must paint. This is why we are divorced."

"No," Frida answered gently. "I am done painting. I have no one to paint for."

Alarmed, Fulang tried to tear the ribbons away from Diego's portrait, but Frida brushed her away.

"Scat!" Frida growled.

Fulang followed her throughout the house, feeling helpless. Frida methodically went from room to room, wrapping her paintings with ribbons. It was clear she did not want to see them. "You remind me too much," she said dismissively. Finally, when Frida came to the portrait of Dismas in his princely burial clothes, she stopped. The neighborhood boy had died young.

"Oh, Dismas!" she cried "You died like every child of mine died." Over the years Frida had tried to have children, but every time she became pregnant she had to have an abortion in order to save her life. Her accident had made it life threatening for her to bear children, but her desire to be a mother overrode any concern for her own safety, and she continued to get pregnant.

She took down the painting from the wall and held it in her arms. She rocked the portrait of Dismas, his eyes closed and his hands clasped across his chest with a pink gladiolus slipped between his dead fingers. "You are my only child now," whispered Frida. "I will have no others."

"Oh, please," Chica purred, as she ran her tongue along the length of her tail. Like a shadow, her black body defied the patch of sun under the window where she lay. Her cold yellow eyes watched as Frida swaying. "This is just ruining my day. How can I get some sleep with her sobbing all the time?"

"Show a little consideration, why don't you?" spat Fulang, as she gathered the butterflies back into their glass box. With small, delicate fingers she carefully lifted a monarch butterfly from the floor. Its beautiful orange-and-black wings shown like sheer gossamer in the light, and tears fell from the monarch as it was returned to the glass box.

The entire house—the chairs, the paintings, the knickknacks and whatnots—seemed to be on edge.

"Even when she's bedridden with pain, she has some hope," observed one of the skeletons hanging from the bed's canopy.

"Diego is such a jerk," added a doll on the dresser.

"We can't just stand around and watch," rattled the candy Day of the Dead skull. "You can't stand around at all," hissed Chica because the skull had no body. The skull's teeth clacked so annoyingly when it talked that she found it impossible to listen to him.

"Very funny, but Skull has a point," replied Fulang. "We can't let this divorce ruin her. We have to bring her out of the dumps."

Abruptly, Frida put down the portrait of Dismas and tore at her clothes. Awkwardly, she undressed, throwing her Tehuana costume into a corner and digging out an enormous pair of Diego's pants from the dresser. They were gray and extravagantly hemmed with two-and-a-half-inch cuffs. The pants ballooned around her as she belted them tightly around her small waist. She pulled on a voluminous crimson work shirt. As she buttoned the front, her body seemed to disappear into fabric so excessive that she seemed engulfed by a deflated hot air balloon. Her neck poked out of the buttoned collar like a chicken peeking out of a hen house. Slowly, she tucked the sprawling shirttail into her pants and began to pull on silk socks with funny little garters to hold them up. She slipped her feet into a pair of black oxfords left over from her school days and sat before the dressing mirror. She picked up a brush and ran it impatiently through her hair. The long black locks fell over her shoulders like a dark waterfall.

"What is she doing now?" clacked the skull in alarm.

"Frida, Diego's clothes don't fit you," said Fulang.

Frida shrugged. "That's the point. Nothing fits me anymore. I have no place."

Chica casually bit the ends of her claws. The skull was unable to make any facial expressions because the bone made of sugar had no skin or muscles to move. Instead, it sat on the dresser with its hollow mouth agape.

Frida gazed critically at her image in the mirror. Finally she moved decisively, bowing her head forward and letting her black strands fall over her face. She picked up a pair of scissors and snipped high on her head, cutting away lengths of hair in large clumps. Within moments nearly all of her long black hair lay scattered on the floor.

"No!" gasped the skull. "I love your hair." For the skull, everything was a crisis.

"Don't worry," suggested Fulang. "This will pass. It always does."

"Well, it won't," replied Frida coldly as she snipped away.

Fulang reached down and began to place the shorn locks on her head. "How do I look, Frida?" She was trying to make light of Frida's actions. "I've always wanted hair like yours."

"It's yours," Frida replied without glancing at the monkey. "I am no longer a woman." She put down the scissors with a decisive crack on the dresser. Then she deepened her voice in an apparent imitation of Diego. "*Mira que si te quisé, fué por el pelo. Ahora que no lo tienes, ya no te quiero.*" "Look if I loved you, it was for your hair. Now that you are bald, I don't love you anymore." She hummed a few notes and almost seemed about to break into song. Instead she picked up an old comb of Diego's covered in hair pomade and ran it through her shorn locks. After a moment admiring the results in the mirror, she scooped more gel from Diego's hair pomade jar and rubbed it into her hair. She combed her hair straight back in the style of Diego's.

"My next conquest will be a woman," Frida said as she grabbed the crotch of Diego's pants like she had witnessed so many men do. "No more men." Though no one would mistake her for a man, Frida had transformed herself as completely as possible from a beautiful woman who dressed in traditional clothes into a strangely masculine woman wearing clothes much too large for her. She no longer resembled the Frida whom Fulang knew. In a way she looked like a reduced, but much more beautiful, man.

Impulsively, Frida picked up a brush and smashed the mirror as if she couldn't stand the image of herself anymore. "Give me that." She snatched the locks Fulang had draped on her head. Then she gathered the remaining hair from the floor and dashed from her bedroom.

"I've got a feeling this isn't going to end prettily," muttered Fulang under her breath.

Frida disappeared into her painting studio at the other end of the house.

"What gives you that idea, genius?" cracked Chica.

"She could be destroying her paintings," clacked the skull.

"She would never do that," said Chica.

"Like she would never cut her hair?" added the skull.

"Shut up, you deformed candy cane, or I'll lick off your face," spat Chica.

"I think it's time we take matters into our own hands," suggested Fulang. "Follow me." She picked up the skull and led them into the studio.

Inside the small and cramped painting studio, shelves lined one wall, while rolls of canvas and stretchers lined another wall. A tall mirror leaned against the wall beside the window. Frida sat in a bright yellow straight-backed chair and carefully draped strands of her shorn black hair over the back of it. She tied others around the legs and rungs. The last of the hair she scattered around her feet. The clumps of hair looked menacing, almost like vines or snakes that would soon entwine her. She arranged the scene as if the image would have to tell the entire story of her desolation after being divorced by Diego. This was the story of her life. She had to get it just right. She picked up a clump of hair and carefully braided it.

With a sense of exhaustion or perhaps inevitability, Frida picked up a paintbrush and began to sketch out the image of herself that she saw in the mirror. If nothing else, Frida was a painter. Eventually she always ended up before an empty canvas, painting.

"This is not so bad after all," said Chica. "At least she's painting." She padded out of the studio.

Still holding the skull, Fulang watched Frida intensely. She had to agree that it was a good sign that Frida was painting, but she still feared for her. In the short span of one day Frida had divorced Diego, weirdly wrapped her paintings in ribbons as if they were mummies, and cut away at her beauty. Now she was painting this image of herself on canvas as if to make the sudden and extraordinary changes permanent.

"How can you destroy yourself so completely?" asked Fulang.

Frida ignored the question. She seemed to be enjoying herself. "This is who I am now. With no child and no husband, I am no longer a woman."

"That's just stupid," snapped Fulang. "I'm getting tired of all this drama."

Frida laughed. After making a few strokes with her paintbrush, she sang again, "*Mira que si te quisé, fué por el pelo. Ahora que no lo tienes, ya no te quiero.*" A <u>wry</u> smile cropped up on her face. She blinked as if the words somehow stung her eyes.

CHAPTER FIVE

Old Big Eyes

"We're here!" shouted Victor.

The bus rumbled into a bustling plaza in the heart of Mexico City. Its brakes sighed as it pulled to the curb. A huge plume of exhaust exploded from its tailpipe and the engine heaved suddenly to a stop. The bus seemed to have gasped its last breath. The passengers spilled out quickly, while Victor and Maria were handed down from the roof by the same passenger who had pulled them up at the beginning of their journey.

"*Gracias, señor,*" said Maria politely. She straightened her skirt and blouse, while Victor took off his straw sombrero and held it tightly in his hands, looking around.

"It's like a circus," gasped Victor excitedly.

"It's totally marvelous," added Maria. "I've never seen so many people. This plaza has more people than our entire village. There must be hundreds of people here."

"Thousands! Millions!" exclaimed Victor as he bounced on the balls of his feet to see through the crowd.

Suddenly rising above the din of voices, a silly little song that their grandmother used to sing to them, about a pesky armadillo that fell in love with an anteater, rang out. In a flash Victor dashed away.

"Victor!" snapped Maria. She watched him disappear between two women arguing over the price of a chicken. Quickly she followed, but Victor was lost in the press of people. "Victor!" she called after him angrily. "Come back here this minute!"

"*¡Oye, amorcito!* You lost your brother?" a boy about her size asked, grabbing her shoulder. He was dressed in a pair of worn overalls with ragged cuffs and a blue work shirt that looked as if it was two sizes too big. He had rolled up the sleeves to his armpits. On his head was a man's fedora that had clearly been discarded by its original owner.

Maria pushed him away and continued through the crowd.

Walking alongside her, the boy calmly said, "He's gone to listen to Viejo Ojoton."

Despite her fear, Maria laughed. "Viejo Ojoton? Old Big Eyes?" she said "That's the funniest name I've ever heard."

For the first time she looked at this boy. He was lean and strong and had a smile that made her want to return it.

The boy grabbed her wrist and pulled her along.

The hoarse voice of Old Big Eyes rang out above the throng. When they got to the edge of the crowd around the singer, there was Victor, and there was Old Big Eyes. The man was blind. His eyes were as large and milky white as dinner plates on his fat face, and he played an old guitar and kicked a big drum to keep time with his foot. Viejo Ojoton sang with all his heart:

"Poor Señor Armadillo, she no like you,
She tell you take your scaly skin and shoo."

Victor was so delighted he joined in to sing the chorus:

"Poor Señor Armadillo, she no like you,
She tell you take your scaly skin and shoo."

When Maria spotted Victor, she slumped with relief.

"He's okay," said the boy. "Children love Ojoton."

Maria smiled. "Do you love him too?"

"Of course!"

"Then you are a boy too, no?" she laughed, flirting.

The boy slapped his chest. "Oh no! Oswaldo is a man of eighteen." He glanced at Maria. "But you must still be a child."

"I am eighteen, too!" lied Maria to impress Oswaldo. She pushed back her hair behind her ears and tried to look older. He politely changed the subject.

"I can tell by your accent that you're not from the city."

"My brother and I just arrived on the bus. My name is Maria." She held out her hand to shake.

Oswaldo gave it a quick shake.

"Well, Maria, you look like an honest person," he said, "and I need an honest person to help me."

"I *am* honest," replied Maria. She prided herself on her honesty. "Once I found two pesos that Conchita Rojo had dropped in the bodega and I returned them to her right away!"

"Exactly!" Oswaldo smiled. "I knew I had found the right person." He stepped away from the crowd, but not so far that Maria would lose sight of Victor again.

Hesitating a moment, Maria followed. "*Sí?*"

The boy pulled a beautiful leather wallet out of his pocket. "I just found this," he whispered, leaning conspiratorially toward the girl. He opened the wallet for a moment and flashed an apparent wad of cash. "It is full of money, and I want to return it to its owner."

"Oh, *sí.*" Maria nodded her head.

"The problem is, I'm afraid one of the bandits in the plaza will steal it from me when I ask people if they've lost a wallet," explained Oswaldo.

Maria glanced around the square. She saw any number of people who looked suspicious. "Why don't I hold it for you then?"

"Wonderful! I wish I had thought of that," the boy said. "Only how can I know that you won't walk away with the money?"

"I won't!"

Oswaldo made a face as if he were thinking hard to solve this problem of trust. He snapped his fingers. "I've got it." He opened the wallet once more. "You let me hold your money while you hold this money."

Maria hesitated for a moment and played with her brooch as she thought.

"Don't worry," Oswaldo continued. "This wallet holds a lot more money than you could possibly have."

Maria thought about this for a moment. How could she lose? She tore into the hem of her skirt and took out the money she had set aside for an emergency along with the few centavos she had in her pocket. It added up to about fifteen pesos, a pittance compared to the thousands in the wallet. "Here."

Oswaldo handed Maria the wallet and took Maria's money. "I'll be right back." He smiled. "I'm sure the owner of the wallet is still around, and I bet he'll give us a reward for finding it." He pushed his way through the crowd and vanished.

Maria clutched the wallet tightly and turned to watch her brother enjoy the music. Victor danced before Viejo Ojoton, and people began to clap. It all felt like a carnival to Maria. She didn't know how she could have been so lucky. Mexico City was wonderful, and she had already made a friend. She was helping him do a good deed and then he would help her.

"Tacos de chorizo! Tacos de chorizo!" a street vendor called. He carried a tray of food and made his way through the plaza.

Suddenly Maria was hungry, but she didn't want to leave the spot where she was waiting. Oswaldo might not find her then. She and Victor had eaten the tamales and the food she had packed on the bus ride, but that was hours ago. She would have to wait for Oswaldo to return with her money. She hoped he would find the owner of the wallet soon.

After another song, Viejo Ojoton put away his guitar and collected the money that people had thrown into his guitar case.

"You are a wonderful singer," said Maria.

"Thank you, dear," he replied. "Why aren't you home? It's dinnertime."

"We just arrived and haven't arranged for a place yet."

"The city is a dangerous place for newcomers. Be careful with your money." The old man tucked his money into his pocket. Leading the way with his cane, he left the plaza for home.

It was getting late, and the plaza was beginning to empty. The vendors were closing their stalls, and people were going home for supper. The booth selling slices of jicama with chile, lime juice, and salt closed. So did the flag stall, the corn-on-the-cob stall, the pork rind seller, the fried banana vendor, and the others. Maria looked around for a sign of Oswaldo, but he was nowhere to be seen.

"I'm hungry," complained Victor when he returned to her side and saw the food stands close.

"We'll eat soon," answered Maria. She craned her neck to see all around the plaza. Slowly, it dawned on her that Oswaldo might not be coming back. She was relieved, however, that he had left the wallet with her. Even though he took her money, she had much more in the wallet.

It was then that she pulled the wallet from her pocket and opened it. When she peered inside, she realized what a fool she had been. Oswaldo had tricked her. He had given her a wallet stuffed with newspaper.

CHAPTER SIX

Advice from Dr. Eloesser

"This is the most depressed I've ever seen her," Fulang said as she carried the candy skull into the living room, "even when she's been in pain." She was referring to the dozen operations Frida had had to strengthen and rebuild the vertebra in her spine and the bones in her foot. Frida would never fully recover from the bus accident.

"Should we call Diego?" clacked the skull.

"Don't be stupid, you brainless confection," snapped Chica, following the two. "He's the reason for all her problems. If he hadn't cheated on her, they'd still be happily married." She stopped in the doorway and casually licked her front paw, as if their concerns about Frida were not really worth consideration. Still, she remained, proving that despite her surface attitude, she was deeply worried.

The skull ignored the cat and shifted awkwardly in Fulang's hands.

"You're being too simplistic," replied Fulang. She set the skull on the coffee table by the couch. "I think we should get help where we can find it. And if that means going to Diego, then so be it."

"Well, we've got to do something," said the skull mindlessly.

A breeze drifted through the room. The ribbons covering the paintings fluttered in the shifting air, reminding them all of Frida's drastic actions. A moment later, as if carried in on this fresh breath, the spider monkey from the garden settled on the windowsill. His long tail stood up behind him like a question mark as he listened. He brushed back the brown and white fur on his head several times and chewed a fingernail. At first the others didn't notice this new arrival, but eventually Fulang felt the monkey's eyes on her back. She turned and saw the new visitor. This was the monkey she'd seen in the garden.

"*Hola,*" Fulang said.

Behind the monkey, a hummingbird darted.

"*Hola,*" the monkey replied.

Noting the hummingbird and remembering it was the Aztec symbol for luck in love, Fulang thought joyously, *This is a sign.* She smiled to herself about the silliness of such a notion.

"I heard what you said before. Can I help?" asked the monkey.

"Oh, spare me," growled Chica. She moved to the couch and reclined on a pillow embroidered with a dove. "What can a *monkey* do?"

The monkey gave the cat a scowl and climbed down beside Fulang to introduce himself. "I'm Caimito de Guayabal." He dipped his head in a self-deprecating way.

"Your name's 'Guava-Patch Fruit'?" She laughed.

"When I was a baby, that's all I would eat," explained Caimito. "So that's what my mother called me."

A sudden, muffled cry interrupted them. This cry was so insistent, its origin soon was clear. A small, framed painting hanging beside the window banged against the wall. Wrapped in ribbons like the others, it spoke like someone bound and gagged.

"It must be suffocating." Fulang quickly unwrapped the bright red and blue ribbons. Caimito joined in unwinding the long strands, while Chica watched the entire affair with disdain.

"It can't suffocate," she spat derisively. "It's a painting, for crying out loud."

"Don't be so literal," replied Fulang.

The full-length portrait appeared from behind the ribbons. It was a portrait of Dr. Leo Eloesser, Frida's surgeon in the United States. In the painting he stood beside a table with a model sailboat. Behind him a sketch of a mother and child hung on a wall. Dr. Eloesser's high celluloid shirt collar seemed to be choking him, and he coughed. "Excuse me, please, but I think what Frida needs is *life*."

"News flash," cracked Chica sarcastically. "She's already alive, which is more than can be said for a lump of pigment like you."

"No, not like that," protested the Dr. Eloesser portrait. "I mean bring some life into Casa Azul. Make her home alive with people. Make her look forward to each day."

"How can we do that?" clacked the skull.

"*Sí*, how?" repeated Caimito. He placed his hand on Fulang's shoulder.

She shrugged off the touch and shot Caimito a withering look. *Typical male*, she thought, *trying to take over.* "Please explain, Doctor," she said, trying to regain control of the moment.

The portrait thought for a moment. "Frida desperately wants

children of her own, but she can never have them. Now that Diego has left, even her fantasies of being a mother are shattered."

"Okay, so now we know how to get Frida more depressed," cracked Chica.

"Let me finish," the portrait replied. "We need to fill Casa Azul with children! This will distract Frida from her sorrow. It will cheer her up. You all know how much she loves them."

"What makes you Mr. Know-it-all?" hissed Chica.

"Hush, Chica," replied Fulang. "Dr. Eloesser has a point. But Frida's nieces are away with their mother. We must find other children. But where?"

He pointed to the mother-and-child sketch behind him that was inside the painting with him. "Frida painted this to remind me of why she wanted to be healed, so she could have children."

The mother in the sketch suddenly awakened from her sleep and looked up. "When she painted me and my child into the portrait, she told me to remind the good doctor of his responsibility to help her become a mother."

The child removed his thumb from his mouth and added, "I heard it too."

"Okay, you bucket of paint, since you have all the answers, how do we fill the house with children?" asked Chica.

Dr. Eloesser smiled. "You will find the answer in a wrestling match between El Corazón and El Diablo."

"What does that mean?" asked the skull.

Dr. Eloesser shrugged. He turned to the mother and child behind him in the painting and they shrugged as well.

"Now you're making *me* angry," said Fulang.

"We'll figure it out together," said Caimito.

"You'll help?" asked Fulang incredulously. "What can you do? You don't even know her."

"I . . . I just want to help." Caimito backed away and then turned and disappeared through the window.

"We shouldn't listen to such silly nonsense from something that isn't even alive," added Chica, nodding toward the painting.

"Thanks for the support," said the skull.

In the other room, Frida began to sing again. "*A mí no me queda ya ni la menor esperanza. . . . Todo se mueve al compass de lo que encierra la panza.*" "Not the least hope remains to me. . . . Everything moves in time with what the belly contains."

In frustration, Fulang picked up the skull and threw it against the portrait.

"Hey!" shouted the skull. "That would hurt if I could have felt it!"

CHAPTER SEVEN

A Magic Trick

The bright afternoon light slowly turned to darkness on the plaza as a full moon rose above. The round yellow disk in the sky beamed like a spotlight from the heavens on Maria and Victor. In the large plaza they felt incredibly exposed. The plaza seemed larger than their entire village, and everything looked different—the paved streets, the huge fountain in the center of the plaza, the tall two and three-story buildings surrounding it, and the many cars and trucks parked everywhere.

"I'm hungry," Victor said. He kicked a piece of trash and sat down on a bench beside the fountain.

"Don't you think of anything but food?" Maria snapped. She was at her wits' end. She couldn't believe how foolish she was for trusting Oswaldo. Now all of their money was gone. She could feel the panic rise up in her throat, almost as if she were going to be sick.

Victor began to cry. Maria sat down beside him, held him in her arms, and rocked him. "I'm sorry, Victor," she murmured. She felt horrible for taking her fear and frustration out on her younger brother. *Why don't I kick a dog now?* she thought.

In a barely audible whisper, Victor repeated, "I'm hungry." He buried his face deeper into her blouse.

"I know, me too, *poquito*," said Maria, lightly stroking his hair, "but we don't have any money to buy food. We'll have to find Mother tomorrow. In the morning I'll ask someone for directions." The two sat there and listened to the strange sounds of the city. Trolleys clanged down the wide avenues while cars and buses dodged one another in a frightening and deadly dance. A loud group of people spilled out of a building a couple of blocks away. Their laughter echoed through the empty plaza.

"Where were we with El Corazón and El Diablo?" asked Maria gently.

"El Corazón just escaped El Diablo's attempt to pin him," mumbled Victor. He tried to act as if he didn't care, but he did.

"*Sí*, I remember." Maria drew in a breath. "Oh yes. El Corazón had just narrowly escaped disaster. El Diablo was so surprised by El Corazón summoning such strength to escape the pin that he was not ready for the flying kick that El Corazón now delivered. El Corazón leaped into the air to deliver his deadly Atomic Earthquake while El Diablo lay helpless as a newborn baby on the mat. As our hero flew in the air, higher than he had ever reached before, El Diablo suddenly marshaled his almost completely exhausted strength to lift his knee and plant it squarely in our hero's stomach as he came down."

"Ugh," groaned Victor, quickly forgetting about his hunger.

Maria smiled. She knew her brother so well. "Instead of delivering the match-ending blow, El Corazón now lay helpless, rolling and writhing in agony on the mat, while El Diablo jumped to his feet and raised his arms to the crowd. He was taunting them, and the crowd responded. Then El Diablo delivered a kick to El Corazón's head. Oh, the match was going badly now. Fortunately El Corazón had the presence of mind to roll out of the ring and onto the floor of the arena. This would give him time to regain his senses."

As Maria described how El Corazón recovered from the brutal kick to the head, she noticed across the plaza a boy emerging from the shadows. In the coming darkness, it was difficult to see him. Maria, who was now on her guard in this dangerous city, suddenly quieted and stood. Thinking it had to be Oswaldo, she tried to steel herself with courage for a confrontation. After a moment, however, she thought it must be someone else. He was playing with some kind of toy.

As the boy strolled through the plaza, she could finally see him clearly. It was Oswaldo, and it was a toy. He was playing with a *balero*, a cup with a ball on a string, trying to swing the ball back into the cup. Oswaldo seemed not to notice Maria and Victor over by the fountain.

"Hey!" Maria shouted. "Where's my money?"

"There you are! I've been looking for you." Oswaldo strode across the plaza.

Maria crossed her arms and looked at him skeptically. "We haven't moved."

Oswaldo held the *balero* out to Victor. "You want to try it?"

"Where's my money?" Maria blocked Victor before he could take the toy.

"Please?" Victor looked up at his sister, pleading.

"It won't hurt him," said the boy, still holding out the toy.

"Where's my money?" she repeated.

"Don't worry. I've got it," said Oswaldo, holding the toy out for Victor.

Victor snatched it from his hand and glared at Maria.

She finally nodded, and her brother began to play.

"It's safe back at my home. I was afraid I'd lose it and then where would you be?" Oswaldo grinned.

"Then, let's go get it."

"Hey, he's a natural," said Oswaldo, watching. He sat down on the edge of the bench.

"I mean *now.*"

Ignoring Maria, he took a centavo out of his pocket and showed it to Victor. Then he closed his fingers around the coin and waved his other hand over it. When he opened the closed hand again, the coin had disappeared.

"Where'd it go?" asked Victor excitedly, forgetting about the balero.

"It's magic!" Oswaldo reached over to Victor's ear and pulled the coin out of it. "Okay. Now make my money reappear," Maria insisted.

The boy stood and bowed dramatically. "Thank you." Then he waved his hand over his head. "Now for my next trick." He pulled a bright red scarf out of his pocket. Then he took back the *balero* and covered it with the scarf. When he pulled the scarf away, the *balero* was gone.

"Wow! How did you do that?" said Victor. "I want to try."

"*Sí* how?" repeated Maria despite herself.

The boy bowed once more. "A magician never reveals the secrets behind his tricks."

Maria suddenly became serious. "Thank you very much for the entertainment, but now give me my money."

"Are you hungry?" asked Oswaldo, changing the subject again.

"*Sí! Tengo mucha!*" answered Victor.

"Let's go to my place and get some tortillas and chorizo. It's just down there." He pointed to an alley off the square.

Maria stiffened, her eyes narrowing. "What are you up to?"

"Dinner and your money back." Oswaldo got up and started walking away.

"Oh, Maria! Please!" begged Victor. He tugged on her sleeve.

"I won't bite," Oswaldo said as he turned back toward them.

Maria had to get back her money. She knew she couldn't trust this boy, yet she had no choice but to follow. She steeled herself to be ready to run if something bad happened. She gripped Victor's hand and hoped it wouldn't.

CHAPTER EIGHT

Backstreets

Shadows inside shadows.

Maria squeezed Victor's hand tightly.

Shadows disappearing into darkness.

Into this darkness they followed Oswaldo. Maria's steps faltered as she entered this night, and Oswaldo turned toward her and smiled.

"Hurry!"

Then he dashed ahead. He dodged the carts, motorbikes, and cars that lined the narrow streets. Maria and Victor could hear the balero clacking in Oswaldo's back pocket, but it was difficult to see exactly where he was.

"He has the eyes of a cat," Victor whispered to his sister.

"I just hope it's a cat and not a lion," replied Maria anxiously. Together they pressed on. After a hundred yards or so down the alley, their eyes adjusted to the shadows and the world beyond the plaza became visible. The buildings lining it had doors that were shut and windows that were dark.

"Yeow!" screamed Maria as she leaped back. A rat was chewing on a crust of bread at her feet. "Maybe I don't really want to see," she muttered, as she and Victor made a wide berth around the creature.

"Hurry!" called Oswaldo again. He was at the end of the alley where it opened onto another street. The lights behind him showed cars driving quickly by.

They crossed the alley, caught up with him, and looked out at all the street traffic. No one seemed to notice the three children out alone. They came quickly to another street and then another. They hurried past small adobe homes and shacks constructed out of discarded crates and sheets of metal. Occasionally they could see into these modest homes, where families would be gathered, eating beans and tortillas. These rooms looked warm and inviting. They reminded Maria of her village and of sitting around the table with her mother and grandmother. Her heart ached to return to those times.

"Wait!" called Victor suddenly. He had stopped in front of a window. Inside, a man whittled small toy tops, the kind that spun when a string was pulled. Beside the man, a boy pulled the strings on the tops, sending them skittering across the packed dirt floor. It was a magical moment to see so many tops dance around the small room at once. The old man glanced out the window. "*Hola!*" He waved.

"*Buendía*," said Maria as she dipped her head respectfully.

"*Buenas noches*," the old man laughed. He was toothless, and his tongue waggled in his mouth like one of those party horns that rolled out when one blew on it.

"That's Menga, the toy maker," explained Oswaldo as he came up behind Victor. "I have one of those back at my place. Come on."

"How far are we going?" She stood firm beside her brother.

Oswaldo laughed. "Not much farther. My father has made a wonderful dinner, and Victor can play with my toys." He brushed Victor's hair with his hand.

Maria nodded. She would get her money and go. There was something strange about Oswaldo that she couldn't figure out. He was both friendly and scary.

"Hurry or the food will be cold by the time we get there." Oswaldo ran on. Maria and Victor followed.

Oswaldo led them down two more streets and then into an alley. As she and Victor followed, Maria lost track of their way. "I have to trust him," she repeated under her breath. "No other choice." She no longer knew how to find her way back to the plaza.

Oswaldo stopped suddenly at a metal shed leaning at a precariously odd angle against an old brick building. Someone had painted No Entry in clumsy letters on it. The door looked as if it had come off the back of a truck. It appeared to be loosely attached.

Oswaldo rapped his fist against the door two times and then waited.

After a few moments, they could hear footsteps and then a voice asked, "Who's there?" The voice sounded old and raspy.

"Me and some new friends," answered Oswaldo.

"Friends?" croaked the voice.

"*Sí.*" Oswaldo nodded reassuringly to Maria and Victor.

A few seconds of silence passed and then the sound of a heavy chain being pulled free was heard. The door had actually been chained shut. A moment later it creaked open. An old man, slightly stooped and with a huge belly, stood before them. "Come in. Come in. I am Oscar." He waved Maria and Victor inside.

As Maria passed Oscar, she noticed that he was dressed rather strangely. The old man wore a maroon brocaded robe and a pale blue tuxedo shirt with ruffles. On his feet were beautifully embroidered gold slippers. He did not look like a man who went out often.

"Oscar, meet my friends Victor and Maria," said Oswaldo.

Maria thought it was odd that Oswaldo would call his father by his first name, but she didn't give it much thought. Everything about this place seemed strange.

"A pleasure." The old man bowed stiffly. His belly nearly brushed the ground. This almost caused Victor to laugh, but Maria pinched him before he could. "Please, this way."

They entered into the hallway and waited a moment for Oscar to replace the chain on the door. He saw Maria watching him closely and explained, "The city is dangerous. We don't want any thieves breaking in."

"I know," Maria replied rudely. "You've already stolen my money."

"We're holding it so it's safe." The old man gave her a look of sympathy. "It's here."

Oscar led them down a long flight of wooden stairs with no handrail. Maria clung to the wall on one side while Victor skipped down like a billy goat.

At the bottom they stepped into a cavernous room that looked like a cave. Huge stalactites hung from the ceiling and stalagmites rose like knees from the floor. The cavern was elaborately decorated with beautiful gold and silver candelabra and velvet drapes. It looked more like an underground palace than a cave. Dozens of candles blazed around the room.

"A secret cave!" exclaimed Victor, very excited.

"It's so beautiful," said Maria, gasping. She had only read of such opulent places in books. The homes in her village contained very simple belongings compared to this cave. "It's like a palace, but it's underground." Then she caught herself. She was here for her money. Nothing more.

"Yes! This is our home," replied Oscar. "I discovered this cave many years ago when I was a boy not much older than you." He stared at Victor, and his gaze lasted longer than was comfortable.

"So what do you think, Oscar?" asked Oswaldo.

The old man smiled. He was missing all of his teeth, so his mouth had the hollow look of a jack-o'-lantern.

Victor looked at his sister. He didn't understand what was going on. But neither did Maria.

The old man turned Victor around. "He's about the right size."

"Size for what?" asked Maria suspiciously. "Where's my money?" Victor ran over to his sister.

"In time, in time," replied Oscar with a wave of the hand. "You must be hungry. I have a hot meal ready." He led them farther into the cavern. At a small stove the old man lifted a lid to a large pot and a fragrant steam rose.

As her stomach responded, Maria felt her uneasiness disappear.

CHAPTER NINE

Dinner and a Story

When Oswaldo rolled out a cart stacked with wooden blocks, Victor broke into a huge smile. The two of them began to build a city of blocks.

"Let's build Mexico City!" Victor said as he dumped the blocks on the floor.

"I have cars too," said Oswaldo.

"Really?"

"And a fire engine." Oswaldo carried a crate from the corner of the cave and emptied a dozen cars and a beautiful red fire engine.

"Wow!" Victor grabbed the engine. It had a real bell. He rang it and pushed the truck all around the room.

Maria shivered. She couldn't help liking Oswaldo, especially the way he played with Victor, but she still didn't like that he hadn't returned the money. She held back and remained by the stairs.

Oscar stirred the large pot of beans. It smelled of spices and roast-ed peppers. He ignored his two visitors as he warmed tortillas and chopped onions.

Maria began to feel silly standing at the edge of the room while everyone else seemed so relaxed. Quietly, she edged her way into the room. "This place is beautiful," she cautiously admitted. "But I still need my money." She felt she was being strong by not wavering on this issue.

Oscar dipped in a slight bow. "Of course." He took a box from a cabinet next to the stove. He counted out Maria's money from a stack of pesos. "I try my best to make a nice home for Oswaldo," said Oscar, ignoring Maria's embarrassment as she hurriedly shoved the money into her pocket. Oscar took a spoonful of grated cheese that was already on the table and rolled it inside a tortilla. "Here, my dear." He handed Maria the tortilla. "You must be ravenous."

"*Gracias.*" Maria, grateful to move past the money issue, took the warm tortilla and broke it in two, handing one half to her brother. Victor shoved the entire half into his mouth. Maria gave him a cross look to warn him to watch his manners.

Oscar returned with the steaming pot of beans and set it in the center of the table. "Let's eat!"

Victor dropped the toys and dashed to the table. Oswaldo, grinning, followed him. It was clear that he was pleased to have kids around. Seeing that reassured Maria.

"I'm starving!" announced Victor as he grabbed a tortilla.

Maria quickly slapped his hand. "Watch your manners."

Victor glared at his sister and then looked to Oswaldo.

"It's okay," reassured Oswaldo, and Victor picked up the tortilla again.

Maria didn't like how comfortable Victor was already getting here. He and Oswaldo had barely met, and Victor was acting as if they had been friends for years. She made a mental note to speak with her brother when they were alone about trusting strangers.

Oscar ladled a heaping portion of beans on Maria's plate. "Have you been in Mexico City before?"

"*Muchas gracias,*" said Maria. "No, this is our first time."

"Well, then Oswaldo must show you the city!" Oscar passed the tortillas and cheese.

"*Sí,* we will go everywhere tomorrow," added Oswaldo. He took a large bite of a tortilla laden with beans. "We'll go to the great plazas. We'll see the murals of Diego Rivera. His great paintings tell the story of the people. And we'll go to the zoo and see the wild animals!" He roared like a lion, and everyone laughed. "Then there's always a puppet show at the plaza. You'll have to see that!"

"Yes!" shouted Victor excitedly. He then took bite of beans. "This is as good as Mama's."

"You are eating like one of those wild animals at the zoo," cut in Maria. Victor's comparison of their mother's cooking to this meal angered Maria and reinforced her resolve to find their mother the very next day. Despite her feelings, Maria did not forget her manners. She turned to Oscar. "This meal is very delicious."

"You honor me with undeserved compliments." Oscar bowed his head. "And where is your mother?"

"We are here to find her," explained Victor. "Our grandmother died, and we've come to be with Mama."

"Do you know where she is?" asked Oscar. He leaned back in his chair, paying more careful attention to the boy.

"*Sí,* Maria knows. Don't you, Maria?"

"We're going to our mother first thing in the morning," said Maria. "So we won't be able to see the city with you, Oswaldo." She looked down at her plate and pushed the food around so she would not have to make eye contact with anyone. Even though her instincts told her to be careful with these people, she was embarrassed for acting rudely.

"I will help you find your mother too," said Oswaldo. "Eat up! There's lots." He shoveled a forkful of beans into his mouth and smiled goofily.

Maria laughed. She did so want to see Mexico City with Oswaldo. "Well, perhaps we could see some of the city first."

"Yeah!" shouted Victor.

Maria and Victor filled their plates a second time.

"That is a beautiful brooch," Oscar said as he leaned across the table to look at it closer. "It's at least a hundred years old."

"It was my grandma's," Maria said proudly. She unconsciously put her hand over it, realizing how this looked to Oscar, who smirked. She scolded herself for not putting the brooch out of sight.

"The silver is exquisite," he said, and then finished his dinner in silence.

After dinner Oswaldo and Oscar cleared the table.

"Let me help," said Maria, picking up her plate.

Oswaldo began washing the dishes, and Maria picked up a dish towel and started drying.

After a couple of minutes, she asked, "Have you always lived here?"

"As long as I can remember," he replied. "Oscar . . ." His voice drifted off as if he was thinking of the exact words to use. "Oscar has been good to me. He has taught me everything."

"Haven't you been to school?"

"No. Oscar taught me to read." Oswaldo's eyes darted across the room toward him.

Maria glanced over at the old man. He held the newspaper as if he were reading, but he actually seemed to be listening to their conversation.

"I can't wait to take you to see the murals of Diego Rivera," the boy said, changing the topic. "It's my favorite thing to do."

"Well, we have to go," Maria said when the dishes were done. "We'll see you at the plaza in the morning."

Oscar stood. "Oh, I wouldn't think of it!" He came over and took Maria's hand, and led her to the couch. "Please, I would be offended if you left now and did not stay the night."

"No, this is not possible," Maria replied, backing away. "Come on, Victor."

Victor looked up from the blocks. "Awwww, Maria, pleeeeaasse."

"There is plenty of room. You and your brother can sleep on the couch," explained Oscar. "Then in the morning, once you're rested, you can find your mother."

"We'll help you," promised Oswaldo. "You don't want to sleep in the street."

Maria didn't know what to say. She didn't want to spend the night in the street, but she wasn't sure if she could trust Oswaldo and Oscar. Finally she decided Oswaldo would be a real help in finding her mother. Reluctantly she agreed. "Just for one night. You are very generous."

"*De nada.* It is nothing," replied Oscar as he brought a blanket over to the couch.

"I'm sleepy." Victor yawned as he plopped down in the middle of the couch.

"Then it's time for bed," said Maria with finality.

She pulled the blanket over Victor and climbed under next to him. Victor curled up beside his sister and asked for a story.

After Maria gathered her thoughts for a moment, she began again the story of the epic battle between the great wrestling warriors El Corazón and El Diablo. "If you remember, El Corazón was lucky enough to roll out of the ring just when that devil thought he had the match won. Well, El Corazón recovered quickly and climbed back onto the ring apron; but before he could climb through the ropes, El Diablo smashed his forearm into our hero's face. Then he began to choke El Corazón on the top rope. The referee tried to stop this terrible breach of the rules, but that evil one simply flicked the referee away like a flea. The referee was not large at all. In fact, you might remember him from when he used to be a midget wrestler. This referee was tossed backward and landed on his head. He was out cold."

"Oh no!" cried Victor.

Maria glanced up and saw that Oswaldo had come over and was sitting on the floor beside the couch. She made room for him and he sat beside them. Inspired by her audience, she continued excitedly. "Oh yes! It was horrible. But it was about to get even worse. While El Diablo choked our hero on the ropes with his arm, he used his free hand to unlace El Corazón's mask. As you can imagine, the arena went crazy. People started throwing things into the ring to stop El Diablo. No one wanted El Corazón to experience the cruelest and most damaging humiliation in all of wrestling. . . . to be unmasked."

"He must be stopped!" said Victor as he balled his hands into fists.

"Oh, he must, but he won't," Maria continued. "El Diablo quickly grabbed the back of the mask and tore it away. El Corazón cried in pain. It was as if the bright lights of the arena were actually hurting him. El Diablo was so enthralled by his triumph that he let El

Corazón go and danced around the ring holding the mask high in the air for all to see. And El Corazón stood on the ring apron, humiliated. He tried to hide his face, but he was coughing so much from the choking that he could not. And when he finally looked up, everyone in the arena gasped. El Corazón was no ordinary man. He was Quetzalcoatl, the ancient Aztec god of life. He had returned to Mexico to save it from such evil as El Diablo, but now his secret had been exposed. It was the same thing that happened to Samson when his hair was cut."

"I know that story," interrupted Victor. "Samson had his long golden locks cut off and he lost all of his great strength."

"And this is what happened to El Corazón. He seemed to shrink before everyone's eyes," said Maria sadly. "Fortunately, El Diablo was so drunk on his triumph, he forgot all about our hero. Instead, he was shouting at the fans in the arena and taunting them."

"Have you ever been to the wrestling matches?" Oswaldo suddenly said.

"No," answered Victor. "We read about them in the paper every week."

"Why don't I take you then," said Oswaldo.

"Really?" Victor turned to his sister. "Oh, please, Maria, can we?"

"We're going to find Mama tomorrow," insisted Maria. She folded her arms.

"Oh, please, please, pleeeeeeaaaaaasssse," begged Victor.

"I can help you find your mother the next day," suggested Oswaldo. "You really should see Mexico City and go to the wrestling matches. There is nothing like it." Oswaldo almost seemed too eager to keep them near.

CHAPTER TEN

No Hope at All

"You must stop this," insisted Fulang, as she hung upside down by her tail from the canopy of Frida's bed. Frida lay propped up by pillows with a small canvas on her knees. Despite being bedridden with pain, she was continuing to paint her self-portrait as Diego. "You need to cheer up and forget about this nonsense."

"You're a lot of help," grumbled Chica from her perch on the credenza across the room. She chewed a claw on her back paw. "Maybe you should talk to the painting again. A lot of help he was."

"Go away," said Frida without looking up from her painting.

Fulang lowered herself onto the bed next to Frida. "Not until you get out of bed."

Frida, who was intent on the brushstrokes that made up the shadows in the crease of the voluminous pants, lifted her brush and painted Fulang's nose red.

"Hey!" Fulang fell back onto the floor, quickly wiping her nose on the bedspread.

Frida picked up a thin horsehair brush and dipped it into a gob of black oil paint she had squeezed from a tube onto her palette. She wiped the brush gently on her sleeve and began to paint in long black strands of hair like the ones she had shorn earlier in the day. With each brushstroke she arranged the strands around her in the portrait. Some were draped on the chair leg while others were strewn about the clay-colored floor. With a flick of her wrist the brush wound hair around the chair's back. The perspective in the painting was so off-kilter that in some places the hair seemed not to lie flat but to dance off the floor.

"I can't stand this," protested Fulang. She pointed at the painting. "You're erasing yourself. There is no inkling of yourself in this portrait. It's as if you want to commit suicide."

Frida smiled and was suddenly more animated than she had been all day. "That's not a bad idea."

"No!" Fulang waved her arms as if she could obliterate the thought.

Frida put down her brush. "I cannot paint with all of you staring at me."

Defeated, Fulang picked up the Day of the Dead skull sitting on the bedside table and left. Chica followed.

"And shut the door!" Frida shouted after them.

Chica pressed her paws against the open door and slammed it shut. "Let her stew. She'll feel better tomorrow. She always does. Besides, she's painting and that can't be anything but good." A light breeze riffled through Chica's fur.

Fulang wasn't convinced. "But look at what she's painting. She has never mutilated herself by cutting off all her hair and putting

on men's clothes. This is much more serious than just physical pain."
In frustration, she did a flip in the air. Sometimes it was so hard for
monkeys to remain still. "This painting is different from her other
portraits. In those she still keeps her basic self. She expresses the pain
she's feeling, but through it all she's still Frida and still a woman. In
this portrait she's someone else."

"She's Diego," added the skull helpfully.

"Right." Fulang glared at the skull. "You are truly stupid,
aren't you?"

"*Sí*," clacked the skull.

"Okay, back to my point. It's as if her self is gone. Diego has
overwhelmed her. It's as if with Diego gone from her life, Frida no
longer exists."

"You'd think it would mean the opposite," suggested Chica.

"There's no logic to it," concluded Fulang.

"El Corazón and El Diablo," murmured the portrait of Dr.
Eloesser.

"Oh, shut up," snapped Fulang. The stress of Frida's depression
was getting to her.

Suddenly, a loud bang from the backfire of an automobile interrupted the discussion. Chica looked out the window and saw a
brand-new white Packard. "Diego's here."

"I hope he doesn't make it worse." Fulang went to the door and
opened it.

"It can't get any worse," replied Chica.

"What's wrong?" Diego stood before them with his arms full of
flowers—beautifully scented bright red gardenias. With his immense

size he looked somewhat comical, like a flower seller's cart set up for business in one of the plazas around town.

"Stop buying that cheap gas at the store," spat Chica. "It'll ruin your car."

"Oh, it's not so bad," replied Diego as he stopped on the doorstep. "Why do you look so worried?" He saw that Fulang's tiny face was squinched up even more than usual.

"They water it down. That's why your wonderful new car coughs." Chica turned and shot her tail straight up, showing Diego her behind.

"What's her problem?" asked Diego. He squeezed through the door and into the living room.

"Oh, she's worried about Frida but won't admit it," explained Fulang.

Chica stuck out her tongue at Fulang.

"Frida? Something's wrong with Frida?" Diego dashed through the house to her bedroom but stopped at the closed door.

"Wait!" shouted Fulang, following behind him and almost getting stepped on in the process.

Bang. Bang. Bang.

Pause.

"Frida? Are you in there?" called Diego. A trail of stunning red gardenias spilled through the house. Diego held only two stems.

"She won't answer," replied Chica, who wound her way through his legs, rubbing her flanks against his pants legs.

"You've got to help her," clacked the Day of the Dead skull. "I think she is preparing to kill herself."

"What?" gasped Fulang.

"*Sí,* she has destroyed everything that she cherishes. She has cut her hair and torn her Tehuana costumes. She has wrapped up all of her paintings. What does she have left?" The skull tried to hop to the edge of the table. He went too far and tumbled off.

Diego picked him up and looked him squarely in the eyeholes. "You really think so?"

Trying to regain his dignity, the skull explained. "Of course. She is painting a self-portrait that is no longer herself. Why would she do that? She is killing the memory of herself before she takes her life."

"Don't be a fool," hissed Chica. "Diego, don't listen to that mindless piece of confection. She'll get through this."

Bang. Bang. Bang.

"Frida! Open this door now!" commanded Diego.

"Go away!" said a faint voice through the door. "Go back to those whores you call artists' models."

Diego staggered back as if he had been hit. "It's all my fault. I just wanted to help her . . . to make her be the great painter she should be." He tossed the remaining gardenia stems across the room and collapsed on the couch. With his face in his hands, he sat there, the springs creaking under his weight. After a minute, however, he sat up and smiled. "I know what."

"What?"

"She needs some joy in her life." Diego stood quickly and strode over to Frida's studio door. "Frida!"

"Go away!" A pause. "Better yet, send one of your whores to me. I need someone to warm my bed."

Diego swung open the door. He stopped short at the sight of her hair. "What have you done to yourself?" Before she could yell at him, he said, "No matter, we're going to the wrestling matches tonight." He pointed at her. "Be ready at six thirty."

"I'm not—"

"No arguments," cut in Diego. "You love the wrestlers, and it will cheer you up." He spun on his heels and marched out of the house before Frida could reply.

Frida stared at the doorway where Diego had stood. A small smile slowly emerged on her face.

A moment later Diego returned with a laundry bag. "Oh, I almost forgot. Here are my clothes." Then he walked over and examined Frida's portrait of herself as Diego. "Not bad," he observed. "You really capture the agony of loss. I love the way you've entangled the strands of hair. You're right that things aren't so simple." He pointed at the clothes in the painting. "Just make sure that you don't completely obliterate yourself. Then the painting will lose all of your soul."

As Diego left, Frida started separating the whites from the colors. She began to sing to herself.

"*Díos mio*," sighed Fulang. "I hope Diego is right." She started to go around the house and pick up the gardenias that Diego had dropped. They were so beautiful and smelled so sweet. It made her want to cry. She wished so much that one day she would be loved like this.

"Find El Corazón and El Diablo," called Dr. Eloesser from his portrait.

"He's got a point," the skull said from a cushion on the couch where Diego had dropped him.

"And what point is that, sugar brain?" grumbled Chica from a patch of sunlight below the window to the garden.

"Well, it's the only thing we haven't done," replied the skull.

Fulang suddenly dropped the flowers she was holding. "No, it's not." She leaped over to the desk and opened the drawer. "We haven't spoken to the one person she'll listen to." She pulled out a piece of paper and a pencil. "If Diego's plan doesn't work, maybe this one will."

"The real Dr. Eloesser!" cried the skull.

"Right. Now help me write a letter," said Fulang. "How do you spell *doctor*?"

"How would I know? I'm a cat," replied Chica as she sat right on top of the sheet of paper.

Fulang pulled the sheet out from under her and began to write as best she could.

> Deer Doktr Ellesser,
> Pleez com fasst. Frida sik.
>> Yurs,
>> Fulang, Chica & Skull

"Okay," Fulang said as she folded the letter. "Who has an envelope?"

"What do you think? That I have pockets?" said Chica.

The skull laughed.

"Enough with the jokes." Fulang took an envelope out of the drawer and slid the letter inside. She opened Frida's address book and copied Dr. Eloesser's address in San Francisco. "I'll mail it right away." The monkey leaped out of the window and over the wall to the garden. She ran along the sidewalk to the mailbox at the corner. Scaling the side of it, she read a poster pasted there.

The Greatest Living Wrestler
El Corazón
Versus
the Mean and Evil
El Diablo
Tonight 7 PM
Mexico City Arena

She dropped the letter in the slot, climbed down, and ran home. She knew where she was going that night.

CHAPTER ELEVEN

A Thief's Life

"Watch this!" Oswaldo winked at Maria and Victor. The three of them were on the busy avenue. Oswaldo had told Maria and Victor that he was taking them to breakfast at the plaza. To Maria and Victor that meant he was going to buy breakfast. To Oswaldo it meant something entirely different. Before they got far, Oswaldo started fooling around. He did a cartwheel. When he landed on his feet, he stumbled into a man in a suit who was walking down the street. "Oh, excuse me, *señor.*"

"Watch where you're going," barked the man, and he went on his way.

Once the man was out of sight, Oswaldo held up a pocket watch on a gold chain. "I *was* watching." He laughed.

"You can't do that!" exclaimed Maria, trying to suppress her own laughter. "Return it immediately."

"That's incredible!" added Victor. "Can you teach me how to do that?"

Maria turned white. "No, you don't. Our mother taught us not to steal." She was struggling to keep her mother in the forefront of her thoughts. But the excitement of being with Oswaldo and exploring this amazing city overrode any sense of responsibility. This was her chance to see the world, something her mother would never let her do.

"Come on! Are you hungry or not?" Oswaldo called. Victor followed, but Maria stood her ground. Oswaldo and Victor ignored her and disappeared around the corner.

After a moment Maria got nervous and dashed after the boys. "Wait!" When she caught up with them, Oswaldo motioned her over. *It's as if he owns the city,* thought Maria.

"See that fruit stall over there?" Oswaldo pointed across the plaza. A man was selling a sack of avocados to a woman. There were other customers sorting through the plantains and guavas.

"*Sí,*" replied Victor. He was excited to be included.

"Ask that man if he has any mangoes."

"Why?" Maria was suspicious, but she was willing to do just about anything Oswaldo suggested. It was so liberating.

"Don't you want breakfast?" asked Oswaldo innocently.

Maria laughed. "I'm starving!" Glancing back at the boys, she crossed the plaza quickly. At the fruit stall she said, "Excuse me, *señor,* but do you have any mangoes?" She couldn't suppress her giggles.

The fruit seller spun on his heel. "Who said that?" The fruit seller was a short, round man in worn overalls and a dirty white T-shirt. His head sat on his shoulders like one of his melons. When he saw Maria, he gave her a long, distrustful look. "No mangoes. Some thief stole my whole shipment yesterday."

Maria started to sympathize with the man, but before she could get out any words, Oswaldo and Victor had stolen armfuls of fruits and vegetables.

"Hey!" shouted the seller. "Stop them!" He took two steps after them but quickly realized he wasn't going to catch the thieves. He also knew that if he left his stall unattended, it would be stripped bare by the time he returned.

Maria froze, then quickly recovered and started to dash away. But the seller grabbed her by the arm.

"Oh no, you don't!" He pulled her back to the stall. "That was the same thief who stole my mangoes. You're in with him. I know it."

Maria had to think quickly. She tried to yank herself free, and she shouted, "Help! This man is trying to kidnap me! Help! Police!"

A crowd quickly surrounded the fruit stall.

"No! No!" said the fruit seller as he let go of Maria. "She's the thief. It is I who want the police." Before he could finish the sentence, Maria had slipped through the crowd. Laughing, she ran back the way they had come. This was the most excitement she had ever had in her life.

Oswaldo and Victor waited two streets over. They tried to eat bananas but were laughing so hard that the fruit shot out their noses.

Maria tried to look serious. She didn't want to teach Victor that stealing was okay. "You think it's funny, huh? That was the man you stole—" But she couldn't keep a straight face and burst into laughter along with them.

Oswaldo bent over laughing. "I couldn't help it," he giggled. "It was too funny not to do."

"Stop it," said Maria. "I can't stop laughing."

Victor snorted banana through his nose again, he was laughing so hard. That caused everyone to break into even greater peels of laughter.

Finally Maria got control of herself. "As soon as we find our mother, we will pay that poor man back."

"Why?" objected Victor.

"It is wrong to steal," answered Maria. She knew she sounded like her grandmother, but since her grandmother was dead, someone in the family had to be responsible. She knew she couldn't just let Victor become a thief. She sat down on the curb next to Oswaldo and Victor and sorted through the apples, cucumbers, and tomatoes they had stolen.

"But it was fun, wasn't it?" asked Oswaldo rather shyly. He seemed embarrassed.

Maria took a bite of a juicy tomato. Pulp spilled down her chin. "Oh, this tastes so good." She sighed. She looked at Oswaldo and shrugged.

He rolled back, laughing.

"Oh, God is going to punish us," Maria said, full of delight.

"Follow me," said Oswaldo as he suddenly jumped to his feet and headed down the street, leaving the food behind.

"Where?" called Maria after him as she scrambled to pick up the discarded banana peels and apple cores to place in a garbage can. At this moment she felt so free of rules she would follow him anywhere.

"Come on! It's a surprise." Oswaldo skipped a few yards. Then he hopped up on a wall and walked along the top as if he were a tightrope walker.

"Let's play follow the leader," said Victor. He clambered onto the wall and did exactly what Oswaldo was doing.

"Maria, don't spoil the fun," shouted Oswaldo.

She stepped up onto the wall and followed them. "Where are we going?"

"It's a secret." Oswaldo grinned.

"I love secrets. Tell me. Tell me. I won't tell anyone!" shouted Victor.

"But then it won't be a secret anymore," replied Oswaldo. He waved them along. "Down here." Oswaldo led Maria and Victor into a large building with a brass plaque on the front that read Ministry of Public Education. Inside the ministry were three stories of open hallways surrounding a huge courtyard, and each hallway was painted with a giant mural.

"Holy cow!" gasped Victor. He was staring at a mural of Indians working the fields and mines. "This looks like home." In another hallway the mural depicted a workers' meeting. "This is a painting of the revolutionaries returning land to the *campesinos*," said Oswaldo. The opposite hallway showed Indian children being taught in an open-air school.

Oswaldo dashed across the courtyard and pointed to a giant of a woman with a large round body handing out rifles to the *campesinos*. "I've always thought this is what my mother looked liked."

As Maria caught up with him, she placed her hand gently on Oswaldo's shoulder. "You never knew your mother?"

"No. I don't remember anything except Oscar," explained Oswaldo.

"Is he really your father?"

"I'm not sure. He says he is, but sometimes I imagine that my real father is a rich man who has lost me and is looking for me." Oswaldo paused. "And someday he will find me."

"Maybe he's the great Diego Rivera!" shouted Victor suddenly.

Oswaldo glanced at Victor and looked as if he was about to cry. Then he pushed Maria and ran through the courtyard toward the exit. On his way out, he grabbed the security guard's baton and lightly whacked the guard on the butt. "You missing this?" he shouted, waving the baton as he dashed out of the building.

"Hey!" shouted the guard, running after Oswaldo.

"He can be such a pig!" said Maria with exasperation. Then she and Victor quickly followed. Without Oswaldo they'd be lost.

CHAPTER TWELVE

Wrestle Mania

"Programs!"

Two huge spotlights swept the sky.

"Hot tamales!"

A mariachi band played traditional music. A dozen men dressed in traditional gaucho outfits played guitars and brass instruments. A woman in a beautiful, flowing red dress danced and sang.

"Programs!"

Crowds of sweaty people pressed toward the turnstiles at the entrance to the arena.

"Popcorn!"

Oswaldo hung back by the parking lot with Maria and Victor. They waited between two cars.

A slight chill descended on the early evening. Maria wrapped her arms around herself and suddenly became self-conscious about her clothing. After two days of travel and living in the streets, her beautiful Tehuana costume was dingy and stained. She hadn't combed her hair since she had left her village, and it was knotted and tangled.

She held it back with a ribbon she had taken from the skirt of her costume. But the way Oswaldo looked at her made her insecurities disappear.

As they waited, Oswaldo took Maria's hand in his.

Maria smiled back at him. Suddenly she wanted to kiss him. She had never kissed a boy before, and, impulsively, she wanted him to be the first. But she was too shy to actually act on it.

"You know," Oswaldo said, "I lied to you yesterday."

"You did?" replied Maria, pulling her hand away from his.

"*Sí.* I am only fourteen, not eighteen. Or at least that's what Oscar tells me. I'm not really sure."

"Is that all?" Maria laughed. She squeezed his hand. "I like fourteen-year-olds better than eighteen-years-olds, especially since I'm fourteen myself."

All around, crowds of people dressed in their best clothes lined up to enter the arena.

"I can't wait to see what it's like inside," said Maria. She tried to imagine what it looked like. "The largest building I've ever been in is the church in my village. And that can't even hold the entire village!"

"It must hold a million people," blurted Victor.

"Well, not quite, but close," replied Oswaldo.

"I know we should be looking for Mama, but I wouldn't have missed this for the world. This has been the best day of my life."

Oswaldo beamed.

"The bus ride around the city was magical," bubbled Maria. "And now we're going to see the real El Corazón and El Diablo, not just a description in the newspaper or illustrations in comic books."

"I can't wait to see El Corazón's Flying Suplex in person," Victor said excitedly as he smacked his fist into the palm of his hand.

"Hold on a minute," said Oswaldo. "First we have to find tickets."

"You don't have tickets?" asked Maria, confused. "We don't have enough money to buy tickets." Her hopes of seeing a live wrestling match were quickly disappearing.

Oswaldo shot them a marvelous grin. "Don't worry. This is where the fun starts." He turned to Victor. "Hey, little fella, you think you could get us some tickets?"

Victor looked at his sister nervously. "I don't know," he said hesitantly.

"It's easy. See that man in the red *guayabera* shirt?"
Victor nodded.

"He's drunk, and his ticket is sticking out of his back pocket."

They watched the hugely fat man staggering by a lamppost.

"But he has only one ticket," objected Maria. "I don't like stealing a ticket. Let's come back when we have the money."

"We only need one ticket," explained Oswaldo, ignoring Maria's objections. He put his arm around Victor. "The great Oswaldo can turn one ticket into three." He slapped his chest proudly and then looked down at Victor. "Now, go on." He pushed Victor out from behind the car.

Maria panicked. This wasn't what she thought was going to happen. "Victor, get back here right now."

Victor glanced at his sister and then at Oswaldo. "I can do this, Maria," he said, scowling.

He ran across the parking lot and scooted up behind the drunken man. As the man staggered toward the arena, Victor reached out his hand and grabbed hold of the ticket. Just then the man reached back and clasped Victor's wrist.

"Who is this?" The man spun around with amazing speed for someone so large.

"Victor!" screamed Maria. She turned to Oswaldo for help, but he looked frozen. Then he turned to her and said, "Sorry." He ripped the silver-and-turquoise brooch off her blouse, and was gone. She could see the top of his head bob between the cars as he ran farther and farther away.

CHAPTER THIRTEEN

A Good Deed

"Hurry, Frida!" shouted Diego.

"I'm coming." Frida stood in front of the mirror, adjusting an elaborate headdress to cover her shorn locks.

Delighted with Frida's change of mood, Fulang sat on Diego's shoulder. "This is going to be so good. I'm glad you thought of it."

Diego patted Fulang on the head.

"How do I look?" Frida stepped into the living room wearing a traditional Tehuana costume and a headdress that looked as if it came out of a Renaissance painting.

"Wonderful!" Diego set Fulang on the couch and took Frida's arm. "We have to go or we'll be late."

"But I'm coming too," said Fulang.

"No, dear," Frida answered. "Tonight it is just Diego and me." The two left the house and drove away, leaving Fulang dressed in her own Tehuana costume with no place to go.

"Is she crazy?" cracked Chica.

"What do you mean?" asked the skull.

"Well, this morning she gets divorced and she's suicidal. Now, she's happy and going on a date with the man who just divorced her."

"*Díos mio!*" replied Fulang. "I didn't think of that. They don't sound like the actions of someone in control of all her faculties."

"She's lost her marbles," clacked the skull cheerfully.

"Shut up, moron," spat the cat.

"I'd better follow her to make sure she's okay," concluded Fulang as she rushed out of the house." "Especially since the portrait of Dr. Eloesser said this wrestling match is where we'll find help for Frida!"

Fulang climbed over the wall surrounding the garden and into a tree with branches hanging over the street. She noticed Caimito de Guayabal, the spider monkey, down the street playing tag with two squirrels, but she was more concerned with catching up to Frida and Diego. The street was empty. They were long gone.

A few minutes later a trolley passed under her branch. She took a deep breath and dropped onto the roof, clinging tightly as the trolley made its way down the street. She faced the breeze as the air whipped through her fur and sent her skirt flapping. It was exciting and more than a little frightening to travel across the city alone. She had never done this before. Whenever she had left Casa Azul, she had been with Frida. Now, alone, she drank in the people on the streets coming and going from buildings and getting on and off the trolley. She passed the National Palace, where many of Diego's murals resided. Finally, on the other side of the city, the trolley arrived at the arena.

Fulang leaped from the trolley onto the roof of a parked car. From there she scanned the parking lot for Diego's car. The waves of crowds were moving swiftly into the arena even though it was still early. Hesitantly, she went from car roof to car roof down the line of parked vehicles. Now that she was there she wasn't sure what she was going to do or how she was going to find Frida and Diego. So many people, so much color dizzied her. She didn't know where to look or what to look for. She thought back to the words the portrait of Dr. Eloesser had spoken: "You will find the answer in a wrestling match between El Corazón and El Diablo."

Well, I'm here, Fulang thought, *but I'm not sure how I'm going to get inside.* She felt safe perched on the roof of a car. She scanned the parking lot and the entrance to the arena for a tree. With all these people milling about, she did not want to be trampled underfoot.

Just then she heard something land on the car roof behind her. She spun around and smiled in relief.

Caimito tipped his head and chattered. Since the magic didn't extend beyond the walls of Casa Azul, he couldn't speak words. He did a couple of flips and chattered his concern.

Fulang nodded back. She appreciated his concern but couldn't stop and play. She decided to take a chance. Taking a deep breath, she darted between the legs of the people. Caimito followed close behind.

Before they got very far, a child screamed.

"Victor!"

Fulang and Caimito looked over to where the cry came from. They saw a girl in a Tehuana costume just like Fulang's, but the girl's was dirty. It was clear she had been wearing the same outfit for a while.

The girl was calling to a small boy who was struggling to break free from the grip of a huge fat man. She ran to the boy and pounded her fists on the man's back.

Without thinking the two monkeys dashed after the girl and hopped onto the giant man's shoulders. Then they stuck their fingers in his eyes.

"*Aaaaggghhh!*" screamed the main in pain. He immediately let go of Victor and flung Fulang off. Caimito hung on and continued to claw at the man.

Screeeeeeeeeeech! cried Fulang, landing safely a few feet away.

She didn't know if the children understood her or not, but they did run.

"You dirty monkeys!" yelled the man.

Thump!

The man kicked Fulang, who rolled under a car to safety. Caimito bit the man's ear and climbed into a nearby car. The man tried to chase the two, but they scooted away under other cars until they were back to the street. Together they hopped the next trolley, safe.

CHAPTER FOURTEEN

Cold Alley

No matter how warm the night, it is always cold in an alley.

Maria and Victor huddled closely together between wooden crates stacked behind a department store.

"Well, at least we're rid of that nasty Oswaldo," Maria said, more to convince herself than her brother.

The day had been truly amazing and fun, despite Oswaldo's strange and disturbing behavior. She didn't approve of much of what he did, but it had been thrilling to roam around the city. To have him just abandon them and steal her brooch was devastating. The brooch was the last object she had that had belonged to her grandmother, and now it was gone. All the good that had happened during the day had evaporated by nightfall. She fingered the piece of paper with her mother's address in her pocket. "At least we know where to find Mama." She sighed. "We can get directions in the morning."

"I miss Mama," whispered Victor.

"Get some rest. In the morning we'll find her."

"Do you think we'll find Oswaldo?" asked Victor as he curled up even closer against his sister.

"We'd better not, or I'll give him a piece of my mind," flared Maria. "We need to find Mama, not Oswaldo." She pulled the skirt of her costume down over her legs and wrapped her arms around her brother. "We should have been looking for her all along instead of fooling around with that hoodlum."

"Could you tell me about El Corazón?" said Victor, yawning.

"Sure." Maria thought back to where she had left off. "Remember that El Corazón had just received the worst humiliation any wrestler had ever experienced. His mask was torn off his face, and his real identity was revealed."

"He is Quetzalcoatl, the ancient Aztec god of life, and he had returned to Mexico to save it from such evil as El Diablo; but now his secret has been exposed. It is just like what happened to Samson when his hair was cut," Victor repeated faithfully.

"That's right. Quetzalcoatl seemed suddenly to lose strength, and he began to shrink to the size of one of those sacred Indian statues." She stroked her brother's hair. "Fortunately, El Diablo was celebrating as if he had already won the match. He was taunting the crowded arena while they—"

Bbbthskpt! Victor's snore interrupted the story. He was fast asleep. She would finish the story another time. Now she tried to get some rest. Maria drifted in and out of sleep fitfully, waking at every sound echoing down the alley, jerking awake to strange shadows and wearily dropping off again. The night slowly passed.

At dawn the light crept into the alley like a pale gray veil. She gently shook her brother awake. Together they brushed the dirt of the alley off their clothes as best they could.

"I'm hungry," sighed Victor. They had not eaten dinner.

"Me too," said Maria. "Let's find a café."

"I can steal us breakfast!" Victor said proudly. "Oswaldo showed me how."

"No. We do not steal. Didn't you learn your lesson yesterday?"

Because it was so early, the streets were still empty.

A few blocks away, they rounded a corner and saw an open café with tables out front along the sidewalk. It was busy with early morning customers.

"Look! There's Viejo Ojoton!" cried Victor. At one of the tables sat the old man eating eggs and drinking *café con leche*. Victor ran up to Ojoton. "Are you going to be in the plaza today?"

"Who is that?" asked the old blind man.

"Victor," said the boy, patting his chest. "My sister and I met you two days ago."

"Oh, yes! The newcomers. Did you find a place to stay? Won't you join me for a little breakfast? I don't often have company." He moved his cane out of the way so that they could sit.

As Maria and Victor sat, Ojoton ordered tortillas and eggs for them from the waiter. "Now, why have you come to the city?"

"We've come to find our mother," explained Maria. "She works for a family in Coyoacán." Their eggs arrived, and they ate hungrily.

"Oh, that's not far at all. Just a short trolley ride." The old man sipped his coffee.

"Is the trolley near?" asked Maria.

"A trolley leaves from the plaza." Ojoton reached into his pocket and pulled out his money. "Let me treat."

"Oh no, sir, we couldn't," said Maria weakly.

"Yes, you can," said the blind man.

"Thank you," said Victor, putting his hand on Maria.

Each bill in the wallet was folded differently so Ojoton would know its amount. He laid the money carefully on the table and then re-counted it. When he was done, he said, "Ready?"

"Yes," answered the two.

"I have to get my instruments." Ojoton pointed down the street to his right. "Go two blocks down this street and you'll see the plaza on your left. A trolley should be coming by right away."

"*Gracias,*" said Maria. "And thank you for breakfast. I hope we can return the favor soon."

"Good luck finding your mother." The old blind man made his way in the opposite direction, tapping his cane on the sidewalk as he went.

"Can't we go with Ojoton?" Victor said.

"No, we need to find Mama."

"We'll never find Mama," cried Victor. "Mama is gone like grandma and Papa. I want to go with Ojoton. I don't want to be lost again."

Maria grabbed Victor's wrist and pulled him along down the street.

"Mama's dead, just like Grandma," shouted Victor. "I don't want to go!" He broke free and ran after Ojoton.

"Victooor!" screamed Maria. She ran after her brother, but by the time she reached the corner, he was gone. It was as if he had disappeared into thin air. She ran down to the end of the block. That street was empty too. "Victor!" she called. "Victor! Come back!"

As she searched the surrounding blocks, cars began to crowd the streets and pedestrians the sidewalk. It wasn't long before she was hopelessly lost. Only then did she realize that she should go to the plaza. *That's where Ojoton is,* she told herself, *and that's where Victor will be.*

She glanced around to get her bearings but didn't have a clue where she was. "Excuse me," she asked a woman carrying several bags filled with fruits and vegetables. "Can you tell me where the plaza is?"

The woman didn't stop, but she pointed with her chin in the direction from which she had just come.

Maria ran. As she arrived at the other end of the block, she could hear Ojoton singing.

> "Poor senor Armadillo, she no like you,
> She tell you take your scaly skin and shoo."

She turned and ran down the next block, which opened on to the plaza. A crowd stood in a circle, laughing and singing along with the old blind man's song.

A wave of relief overcame her when she spotted Victor in the audience. She ducked behind an old woman with a cart and circled around the crowd.

As the crowd clapped, Viejo Ojoton strummed his guitar and sang another song.

> *"Esta noche m'emborracho,*
> *Nina de mi corazón.*
> *Mañana sera otro día*
> *Y verás que tengo razón."*

> *"Tonight I will get drunk,*
> *Child of my heart.*
> *Tomorrow is another day*
> *And you will see that I am right."*

"Victor!"

A moment later she heard her brother shout. She rushed over, but not fast enough—Victor was gone.

"Help!" shouted Victor.

Maria bounced on her toes to see through the crowd. She turned to her left. Then her right. Finally she saw him, forty feet away, but he wasn't alone.

Oswaldo was with him, with his hand clamped over the boy's mouth as he whispered in his ear. Victor struggled, but Oswaldo's grip was too strong. He forced Victor across the plaza, and they disappeared down the alleyway they followed the night before.

They passed the toy maker's shack and the other huts and businesses. No one seemed to notice a small boy being marched down the street by a boy twice his size.

Maria dashed after them. "Hey! Let go of him!" she cried as she caught up to them.

Oswaldo spun around and froze. "Maria!"

"Let him go!" she said again.

"I want to help. I promise." Then he let go of Victor and ran.

Maria started after him; but when she heard Victor crying, she turned back.

"It's okay, Victor," she said. "You're safe now. You're with me. And now we can find Mama."

"But he's going to come after me again," sobbed Victor.

"What? Why?" asked Maria.

"That man Oscar sent Oswaldo after me," said Victor. "He said Oscar is waiting for me."

CHAPTER FIFTEEN

Painting the World

The morning after the wrestling match, Frida sat painting in her studio. She held her paintbrush as if it were made of finely blown glass.

"She should be happier," said Fulang, sitting on the windowsill. "She looks depressed."

"How can you tell?" asked the skull.

"She's wearing Diego's clothes again," answered Fulang.

Delicately, Frida articulated the fabric covering her shoulders in her portrait, which sloped toward the edge of the canvas. The folds and creases indicated where the shirt's sleeve and front panel met. With a dab of grayish paint, she brushed in the shadows.

"But she's painting a new painting, not the one with her as Diego," countered Chica, cleaning her face with a paw in a patch of sunlight.

"Why don't you ask me instead of talking as if I'm not here?" cut in Frida.

"Okay. Are you upset?" asked the skull stupidly.

Frida put down her paintbrush and glared at her friends. "For your information, you nosy parkers, Diego is gone. He only took me out last night because he felt sorry for me. He's already sleeping with that pig whose name I won't speak." She picked up her brush again. "I am truly alone."

"More time for painting," volunteered the skull.

"Oh, shut up."

She pointed her brush at her painting. "This is my world. My only world. I won't ever again allow myself to be deluded and taken in by the world outside of this."

Fulang perched on the back of Frida's chair, alternately glancing at the painting and the image of Frida in the mirror that she was copying into her portrait. "This is no good," Fulang finally said.

"What? She always paints herself," replied Chica. "And she always adds stuff that's not really there. How is this different?"

"I don't like you putting this other monkey into it. You don't even know Caimito de Guayabal. He's a good guy." She paused, but Frida didn't respond. "He would never do that. Just the opposite, in fact." She remembered how he had helped her the previous evening. But in the new painting, Caimito was being portrayed as menacing, intent on hurting Frida. A necklace of thorns, like the crown of thorns worn by Christ at his crucifixion, was wrapped around Frida's neck in the painting. Caimito was baring his teeth menacingly and pulling the necklace so that the thorns were digging deeply into Frida's flesh. Fuang turned away. *The painting is a lie. Caimito is gentle, not violent,* she argued in her head. *He is so nice.* She was surprised by her warm feelings toward him.

Ignoring Fulang's distress, Frida set down the brush with gray paint and chose a fresh clean one. She dipped the fine horsehair bristles into bright bloodred oil paint. She went over the bright tears of blood that rolled down the neck of her portrait. She repeatedly glanced into the mirror and compared the way she looked to her portrait. It was important that the likeness be as accurate as possible. Frida was determined to paint everything as if it were real, especially those things that were not.

Lying in a patch of sunlight below the window, Chica raised her head and inspected Frida's effort. "I would have swallowed the hummingbird already. They're no more than a morsel, not worth spending the time chewing." She was referring to the fact that Frida had painted Chica on her left shoulder, holding a dead hummingbird halfway in her mouth. The hummingbird was tied to the thorn necklace like a pendant.

Fulang winced at Chica's comment. She felt so strongly that the world Frida was portraying was wrong, but at the same time she was helpless to change anything about it. "Oh, Frida," she said sadly.

"*Quitate de aquî, creatura!* Beat it, kid!" Frida snapped.

It was only then that Fulang realized the implication of the hummingbird. In Aztec mythology the hummingbird is a sign of luck in love. For Frida to paint a dead hummingbird tied to a necklace of thorns was her way of saying that there was no luck in love. Frida was saying that she was a martyr for love the way Christ was a martyr for humanity. On top of this, to include Caimito in the painting was worse than cruel—it implicated him as being responsible for her suffering. "You can't do this," Fulang finally said.

"It's just a painting," said Chica. "It means nothing." She began to clean her paw with her tongue.

"No, a painting is more than a picture," insisted Fulang. "It might tell the future." Fulang was worried that if Frida painted it, the image of Caimito's cruelty might come true. She didn't want such thoughts to become conscious. Fulang tried not to look at the painted Caimito, who seemed less innocent and more frightening than the real one, more like a wild animal. This was even more accentuated by his contrast to Frida's regal calm in the painting. Frida seemed more like a queen who had come to accept the inevitability of her slow, painful death.

"What, are you a critic now?" replied Chica sarcastically.

"Don't worry, this is my last painting," replied Frida as she added some blood splatters on the blouse. "Should I paint my eyebrows into birds? Crows, maybe?"

Fulang sighed. "That's not what I meant."

The conversation quieted for a few minutes. Frida was barely paying attention to Fulang. The monkey fumed.

Finally Fulang tried another approach. "I like that you are painting your world, but your world is not my world, and I don't appreciate you putting Caimito in there."

"He will only disappoint you like Diego," replied Frida sadly, setting down her brush and turning to her friend. "Trust me on this. Men are worse than pigs. They are only alive to hurt you."

"That's not true for everyone," insisted Fulang. "Perhaps it is just you who needs to avoid men. Besides, you have your painting, and it can be your muse and your companion."

"I will die without Diego," Frida suddenly said. Her shoulders slumped, and she dropped her paintbrush on the floor.

"You have just had bad luck," counseled Fulang. "Focus on your painting. Even Diego says that."

Suddenly, across the room on a desk piled with paints and brushes, Frida's diary flipped open to a sketch of Frida. As if it had not been listening to their conversation at all, the sketch spoke, reciting a list of colors and their meanings, which Frida had written that morning.

> *Reddish purple: Aztec.* Tlapali, *which is the Aztec word for*
> *"color" used for painting and drawing.*
> *Old blood of prickly pear. The most alive and oldest.*
> *Green yellow: more madness and mystery. All the phantoms*
> *wear suits of this color . . . or at least underclothes.*
> *Magenta: Blood? Well, who knows! Just remember that*
> *blood must be spilt. Otherwise Quetzalcoatl, the ancient*
> *Aztec god of life, will want revenge.*

Fulang leaped across the room to the desk and slammed the diary shut. This wasn't about painting anymore. It was about Frida trying to ruin Fulang's budding friendship with Caimito.

Frida stood. Out of nowhere she blurted, "Let's have a Cinco de Mayo party!"

"A party, *sí!*." Fulang was relieved that Frida was perhaps changing her mood. "You love Cinco de Mayo."

"The Mexican Revolution happened the year I was born," replied Frida.

"Liar," spat Chica.

"Well, I should have been," answered Frida stubbornly. "My life is a revolution!" Chica held her tongue. Even though Frida had actually been born in 1907—not 1910—she insisted to everyone that the year of the revolution was also the year of her birth and claimed that she was born of revolution. This was the reason why she did not have to follow other people's rules. She was born to break them!

Fulang began to list all the things they would need. "Invitations, drinks, food, a mariachi band . . ."

"And a giant papier-mâché Judas," added Frida.

"Judas? He's the apostle who betrayed Jesus." Fulang shook her head, dismissing such an idea as ludicrous. "No. He doesn't belong at this party. A Day of the Dead party, yes. A Cinco party, no."

"But he will be there," said Frida. "Right by the front gate to greet everyone."

"That'll make this a celebration of betrayal and mar—" Fulang stopped herself. She didn't like where this idea was going.

"That's nothing to sing about," said the skull.

Fulang pointed at the painting. "That's why you're putting in the thorn necklace. You're the martyr. You actually *believe* that your life is equal to the suffering of Christ."

"Exactly."

"What arrogance!"

"I am what I am," whispered Frida. She retreated to her bedroom, slamming the door behind her. She limped because the pain in her back had been getting worse lately.

CHAPTER SIXTEEN

Lourdes 27

"Eat quickly," said Maria. "I want to get going." By the time she had found her brother and returned to the plaza, it was almost lunchtime. Maria thought they had better eat before they caught the trolley.

Victor took a huge bite of his deep-fried empanada filled with cheese and spicy hot habañero peppers. The cheese and pepper juices dripped down into his lap where a fire-roasted ear of corn rested.

"Mmmmgpha mmgg mffa," said Victor.

"Don't talk with your mouth full," said Maria, handing him a bottle of guava soda pop. Victor drank deeply. She ate her empanada quickly but was more careful about the dripping cheese and juices. She held hers away from her body as she bit.

"It's just amazing," said Maria.

"What?"

"This!" She waved her hand around. "This!"

"Huh?"

"Hundreds . . . thousands . . . hundreds of thousands of people all in one place."

Victor glanced around, unimpressed. "I think I'm ready to go home."

"What? I never want to leave," Maria said. "This is the center of the world. Everything is here, and I don't want to miss any of it." Maria took another bite. "I wish I was one of the beautiful women." She pointed to a couple of women crossing the street dressed in pencil skirts, bright blouses, and high heels. "I wonder what it would be like to work in an office and speak to someone far away on a telephone."

"Yuck! I want to tend goats and grow corn. Then I'll never be hungry."

"Hurry, we have to catch the trolley," Maria said to her brother. She stuffed the last bit of empanada into her mouth. "We can catch it right over here." She looked toward the main avenue to see if any trolleys were coming. "I hope it hasn't come already." She was getting anxious that they might have missed the trolley. What if it only came once a day, like the village bus? "I don't want to sleep in an alley again."

Maria stood and motioned for her brother to get up.

"I'm not done," he said. He bit into the ear of corn.

"Finish it while we walk," said Maria. "We don't want to miss the trolley."

"No," he said. "I want to hear about El Corazón."

Maria crossed her arms and shook her head from side to side. "Don't you want to find Mama?"

"We're never going to find her," mumbled Victor. "Let's go home."

"What? Are you crazy?" Maria suddenly lost her temper. "We *are* going to find Mama. We have to find her. I will not lose her like we did Grandma and Papa." Now Maria stomped her foot. Glaring at each other, the siblings had reached a standoff.

A woman walking down the sidewalk smiled at them, catching Maria's eye.

Maria took that as an invitation to speak. "Excuse me, but do you know where I might catch the trolley to Coyoacán?"

"You're in luck," said the woman. "The stop is right at the corner." She looked over her shoulder. "You'd better hurry. It's coming right now."

"*Muchas gracias,*" replied Maria as she grabbed her brother's hand and dashed to the corner.

Clang. Clang. The trolley conductor rang the bell as the car slowed to a stop.

Maria and Victor boarded and paid the conductor with the last of their money. The trolley was so crowded, Maria held Victor tightly against her as she held onto a strap hanging from the ceiling.

Picking up speed, the trolley lurched down the avenue on its tracks, throwing passengers from side to side. Thinking she might be thrown from the car, Maria held on to the strap tightly. "We could get killed in this thing if we had an accident," Maria said as she watched automobiles and trucks constantly crossing the tracks without warning. People on the street dashed out into the traffic to cross the street when they saw an opening.

Maria prayed quietly that this metal box on wheels would not crash.

"Ouch!" Victor cried as the edge of a briefcase poked him in the face.

Maria turned his face toward her. "It won't take long." But the ride out to Coyoacán was much longer than they hoped and most of it was spent being jostled between other riders, being thrown off balance, and grabbing onto each other and the rail. Finally, as the trolley reached the edge of the city, it became less crowded. Maria and Victor found a seat in the back where the air was foul with a mixture of perfume, aftershave, car exhaust, and sweat.

Once seated Maria turned to Victor and grilled him about Oswaldo and Oscar. "What did Oswaldo say about Oscar?"

"Nothing." Victor paused. "Just that Oscar wants me."

"Did you see Oscar?"

"No," replied Victor.

Maria grimaced. "Oscar said almost the same thing that night we spent in the cave. I wonder what he wants?" Maria patted her brother's knee. "Don't worry. He can't get us now."

The two lapsed into silence.

"Now I can return to El Corazón," said Maria gently.

"Good," said Victor.

"What is surprising about a god is that he can summon strength from places that no human can imagine," began Maria. "And Quetzalcoatl had powers that he was hiding behind the mask of El Corazón. This is the only way to explain how the huge wrestler El Corazón could change into a six-inch stone statue once his mask was removed and still be able to leap up, grab El Diablo by the ears, and throw him from the ring."

Out of the corner of her eye, Maria noticed a man boarding the
trolley. He was toothless and dressed in a wrinkled suit. He sat
directly across from the two children and gave Maria a menacing
glare. This look so unsettled Maria that she forgot her place in
the story.

As the trolley moved down the road, the old man laughed to himself and licked his lips while continuing to stare at Maria and Victor.
After a few minutes of this, both children were extremely uncom-
fortable, so they moved to the front of the trolley.

When the trolley slowed at the next corner, she grabbed her
brother's hand and pulled him off. They spilled out onto the street,
not knowing where they were.

The cobblestone street was deserted. Beautiful plane trees lined
the street and cast dappled shadows on the uneven paving. In contrast
to the heart of Mexico City, the only sounds were birds singing in the
trees and the distant strains of someone playing the piano.

The serene atmosphere of the neighborhood had a calming effect on
the two children. "He's not following us," Maria said, glancing back.

"Are you sure?"

"Yes. This way. There's a street sign up here. We can't be that
far away."

"I hope so," said Victor.

"It seemed as if we'd been riding that old trolley forever." As they
walked Maria glanced around. "These houses are beautiful!"

The houses that lined the street were all similar one-story stucco
homes with flat roofs. They were laid out in the colonial style, U-
shaped buildings with many doors, each one leading to a single room.
All of these houses were whitewashed with painted shutters, except

one. This unique house was painted a beautiful bright blue, enlivened by tall, many-paned windows with green shutters.

Maria noticed the house right away. "It would be nice if Mama lived there." She sighed wistfully. The house was on a corner. When the children approached, they could read the address set in the outer wall on blue tiles. It read Lourdes 20.

"Lourdes!" shrieked Maria. She dug the envelope with the return address out of her pocket. "Lourdes twenty-seven!" Maria read. Quickly she spun around and ran to the house next door. "Twenty-two!"

She dashed across the street. "Twenty-five!" She went to the next house, which was number twenty-seven. "Come, Victor!" Jumping up and down, she couldn't contain her excitement. "It's here!"

Grinning, Victor ran across the street. "We're going to find Mama!"

"Here."

Together, the two children reached for the gate on the outer wall enclosing the property. When Maria pulled on the handle, the gate didn't budge.

"It's locked," Maria groaned. "And padlocked. But someone *must* be there."

Victor banged on the gate and called, "Anybody there?"

Silence.

"Hello?" added Maria.

Silence. No one answered.

Maria shook the padlock. "Why would they put a padlock on the gate?" She noticed that the handle on the gate also had a keyhole, so it must have a lock as well. "They already have a lock. Why the extra protection?"

"Maybe they want to be extra safe," suggested Victor, not realizing what this padlock might mean.

"No, that's not it, because then they wouldn't be able to get in and out easily." Maria hesitated. She didn't want to say what she was thinking. "There must be another way in. Let's look around. Maybe we'll find out that Mama is here and we just have to wait for her." She helped her brother over the wall and then climbed over herself.

On the other side of the wall, Maria froze in stunned silence.

The enclosed courtyard was not just deserted. It had been empty for a while. The grass was overgrown. Ivy crawled like thick, long fingers across the tiles of the patio. Leaves were scattered everywhere. It looked as if no one had been in this courtyard for ages.

"This isn't good," muttered Maria. She knew this meant that her mother was gone, but she wasn't ready to tell her brother.

"Where is Mama?" asked Victor in a trembling voice. His eyes teared up.

"We'll find her," insisted Maria. She scanned the courtyard for any signs of recent activity. There were none. "Let's check the house." She grabbed her brother's hand and stepped away from the wall. "Come."

Dead leaves crunched underfoot. They made their way to the closest door. "Locked," said Maria when she tried the handle. They put their faces up against the window in the door to look inside. The room was empty except for a broken chair and trash.

"Over here," said Victor. He had noticed that one of the tall windows had a broken pane. He reached through the opening and unlocked the window. "Should we go in?"

"You wait here," said Maria. She climbed through and went over to the door. Unlocking it, she said to Victor, "Stay close."

Victor grabbed her hand tightly.

Carefully they went from room to room, hoping to find a clue of some kind. "She had to have been here. We just have to find something that will tell us where she went." What she didn't say was that she feared the worst. Something terrible had happened to their mother.

"Where *is* she?" asked Victor, on the verge of tears.

"We'll find her." She had to be strong for her brother.

She glanced around the room cautiously. The stark reality of this empty house weighed too heavily on her. Her footsteps echoed as she crossed the room to another door. And another.

In the back of the house, the two children came to the kitchen. The space for the stove was empty. A hole in the ceiling indicated where the stovepipe had gone. Maria circled the kitchen, touching the surfaces and feeling the dust under her fingers.

Victor wandered in the opposite direction, opening cupboards at random. He was hungry again and hoping to find something. When he came to the butler's pantry, he opened the door and stepped inside.

"*Aaaghh!*" Victor leaped back, waving his arms. "Spiders!" He had stepped into a spider web.

In a flash Maria was beside him, trying to wipe away the sticky threads. While doing this, she glanced into the pantry and suddenly stopped.

"Oh, Victor . . . Look." In the middle of the pantry floor lay a lace handkerchief, just like their mother's favorite one.

CHAPTER SEVENTEEN

Retablo

The evening descended quickly. The shadows from the trees turned to darkness. A monkey's cry echoed through the quiet neighborhood as if it were a call to the night to be gentle. A black cat strolled down the center of the cobblestone street with a mouse in its mouth. The cat's yellow eyes were slits cutting through the darkness.

A few minutes later the rattle and creaking of wheels announced a tortilla cart before it turned onto the block. The old woman who pushed the cart was tired and moved slowly. As the woman approached the corner of Lourdes, Maria and Victor tumbled over the wall enclosing the home they had just searched. Maria clutched her mother's hanky tightly. Even though they had not found her, she knew her mother had been at this house. This knowledge alone had given her hope.

"Who's there?" called the old woman suspiciously.

"Just a boy on his way home, *abuelita*," called a voice from the shadows up the street.

Maria put her hand over her brother's mouth and whispered in his ear, "Shhhh."

"Do you have any more tortillas?" the boy asked.

"For you, my dear, anything," the old woman cackled. "They were to be my supper, but I will sell my last dozen to you for twenty centavos."

The boy put his hand on his heart. "Five centavos."

"Fifteen."

"Ten."

"Deal." The old woman unwrapped the last of her tortillas and handed them to the boy. Maria strained to hear more. She wasn't certain, but the boy sounded like Oswaldo.

The boy paid and quickly bit into the first tortilla. "Sleep well, *abuelita*," he called after the old woman as she pushed her cart on.

"Quick, or we'll be seen." Thinking fast, Maria grabbed her brother's hand and used the old woman's cart to block the boy's view as they darted across the street. She pulled Victor behind a stand of magnolia bushes.

"But why can't we—?" asked Victor.

Maria put her hand over his mouth once more and whispered in his ear, "Because we don't want Oswaldo to find out and kidnap you again. It's better that no one sees us."

The two held their breaths, listening to the boy stroll down the street eating noisily.

The smell of tortillas lingered in the air. Maria's stomach growled.

The gate at Lourdes 27 rattled. *The boy must be trying to open it,* thought Maria. *But why?* She couldn't see out from behind the bushes.

The boy stood there at the gate and ate his tortillas one by one, humming to himself. Maria and Victor tried not to move. But soon

Victor shifted his weight from one knee to the other. As he did this, his back rose and brushed a branch.

Crack!

The branch broke and clattered to the ground.

Maria wrapped her arms around her brother to hold him still.

The boy paused in midbite. He glanced up and down the street and listened. After a minute he continued chewing. He slowly finished his torillas. Then he strolled back up the street and around the corner, the way he had come.

The tension in Maria's muscles slipped away.

"Is he gone?" whispered Victor.

"Shhh." Maria tried to see through the leaves but couldn't.

For several minutes Maria fingered her mother's favorite lace handkerchief in her pocket and tried not to think why it was left in the empty house.

Together, brother and sister crouched and waited, ready to run if necessary.

The portait that Frida was painting of herself, Chica, and Caimito de Guayabal so troubled Fulang that she refused to enter the painting studio when Frida was working on it. Instead, she sat just outside the door and made snide comments into the room.

"Liar!" shouted Fulang.

"Quiet," snapped Frida. She sat before her portrait, painting dense plants and leaves in the background.

"He came and helped me save two children from a mean man in front of the arena last night," pleaded Fulang.

"This painting is not a picture of real life," explained Frida, exasperated. She massaged her foot to relieve the stiffness. She had told Fulang this many times already. "This is a painting of how the world looks from inside my soul."

"But Chica would never hurt you," argued Fulang. "You know that."

Lying on the couch, Chica ignored this conversation until her name was mentioned. "Hey, leave me out of this."

"It's not whether or not she would hurt me," replied Frida. She sat straight in her chair to align her spine.

"I might," purred Chica. "You never know. Cats aren't so predictable."

"The point is that a painting is not a photograph of reality."

As the two argued, Fulang played with the grass mat that lay in front of the door. Absentmindedly, she had unraveled the weaving and put a piece of grass in her mouth. Suddenly she gagged.

"You okay?" called the candy skull from across the room. He was resting on the table beside the front door.

Fulang waved at the skull that she was fine.

"Hey," the skull continued. "You think you could help me here?"

"You want me to move you?" asked Fulang.

"No," answered the skull. "I was wondering if you could read this letter to me."

"Frida got a letter?" Chica sat up. She loved mail. They all loved mail and looked forward to its arrival every day. But with the tension over the painting, they had forgotten about it.

Fulang leaped onto the small table beside the skull.

"Hey, there's no room for me," complained Chica

"It's from the United States," said Fulang, examining the stamp. "Maybe it's from Dr. Eloesser."

"Give it to me," Frida said, snatching it.

"Read it to us," pleaded Chica.

Frida crossed the room and sat down on the couch. Fulang picked up the candy skull and carried it over. She, the skull, and Chica settled on the back of the couch and looked over Frida's shoulder.

"What's it say?" asked the skull.

Frida tore open the envelope and pulled out a letter. "It's from my friend Clare!" she exclaimed excitedly.

> *Dear Frida,*
> *Ever since I received your tribute to*
> *Dorothy Hale I've been truly upset. I can't give this*
> *to Dorothy's mother. It will upset her too much.*
> *I'm so sorry but I have given it away to*
> *someone else. I can't show this to her mother.*
> *Your friend,*
> *Clare*

Frida pressed the letter against her chest and began to cry.

"What's this about?" clacked the skull.

"Don't you have a brain in your head?" snapped Chica. "Oh, I forgot. You don't."

"Very funny," replied the skull.

"A while ago Clare asked me to do a portrait of Dorothy Hale. You remember Dorothy—jumping out of her apartment window."

"After throwing a party for all her friends," said Fulang slowly.

"I can't believe Clare doesn't like the painting." Frida threw the letter on the table.

"Oh, right," Fulang replied. "You paint Dorothy jumping out of her window and also smashed on the pavement below. Then you have Dorothy as an angel flying above with a banner that reads: The Suicide of Dorothy Hale, painted at the request of Clare Boothe Luce, for the mother of Dorothy. Finally you write an inscription on the bottom: *In the city of New York on the 21st of the month of October, 1938, at six in the morning, Mrs. DOROTHY HALE committed suicide by throwing herself out of a very high window of the Hampshire House building. In her memory this* retablo, *having executed it FRIDA KAHLO.*"

"I let them paint out the words on the banner," protested Frida.

"What mother *wouldn't* be horrified?" Exasperated, Fulang picked up the letter and reread it. "Beside, you promised her it would be a *recuerdo*, like the portrait of Dismas. It was supposed to be of Dorothy lying peacefully for her jouney to heaven, but instead you had to make a *retablo*. You showed her in death—not the memory of her!"

Fulang, Chica, and the skull looked at one another, not knowing what to make of the news or what Frida would do.

Suddenly Frida stood. "Well, what Dorothy did makes a lot of sense." Frida was somber. "When I go, I want it to be like that."

Fulang almost choked when she heard those words. She was already disturbed that Frida wanted to make a giant papier-mâché Judas for her Cinco de Mayo party. Now she seemed to be saying that she wanted to commit suicide after the party.

CHAPTER EIGHTEEN

A Magical World

*B*reathe. *Breathe,* Fulang repeated to herself as she stepped outside into the courtyard. The air had cooled as the sun dipped below the horizon. This was in stark contrast to the stuffiness inside the house. The tension had become so great that Fulang felt as if she were suffocating. She paced across the courtyard and lifted her arms over her head to let more air into her lungs.

"One, two, three . . . " Fulang counted to ten to calm herself. This usually worked, but this time she counted to twenty without much success. In frustration she picked up a stone and threw it at a tree.

"OUCH!"

"Who's there?"

Caimito poked his head out of the branches. "It's me."

"Oh, I'm sorry," said Fulang.

Caimito leaped to the ground. "I didn't think you were in the habit of throwing rocks at sleeping monkeys," he said, rubbing his head and laughing.

Fulang didn't laugh. She just turned to continue her pacing.

Caimito approached her and picked at a flea in her fur. "Is everything all right?"

Fulang stopped and shook her head. "Everything's horrible."

As the night descended, they stood awkwardly and silently, like teenagers who liked each other but were afraid to admit it. Time passed without notice. The birds quieted and the neighborhood seemed to turn in for the night.

"It's just that Frida is so depressed," she finally said. "She's even planning a Cinco de Mayo party that's more a Day of the Dead celebration."

"But Cinco de Mayo celebrates the *birth* of Mexico—as a country free of dictators!"

"It does." Fulang sighed. "What's worse is that Frida has always seen her life as linked to the birth of Mexico. Now she's turning that day into a funeral. And this makes me even more afraid, because I think she is planning to kill herself."

"What?" Caimito stiffened. "We've got to stop her."

"I know that, but how?"

"We must find a way."

Suddenly the soft whisper of a voice made its way over the wall enclosing Casa Azul. It had a soft, beautiful tone to it, almost like music. Fulang and Caimito cocked their heads to hear it better.

"El Corazón stood in the ring, only six inches high, a small stone idol of the god Quetzalcoatl." Like a thread of smoke the words drifted over the wall.

Caimito nudged Fulang and pointed his chin in the direction from which the voice was coming.

"El Diablo, though, lay outside the ring, stunned by the strength of El Corazón, now an Aztec god. He looked up helplessly as Quetzalcoatl drew power from the cheering crowd."

As she listened, Fulang became excited. These were the wrestlers the portrait of Dr. Eloesser had told them about. And it wasn't just the story that she recognized. It was the voice as well. This was the voice of the girl from the arena—the girl she had helped to escape the night before.

Without hesitation she scurried to the wall. She paused to make sure she wasn't hallucinating. Then she sprang to the top of the wall and looked down. Below her, curled under a bush, two dirty street children huddled.

"Please, come in!" a voice called from the other side of the wall.

"I must be sleeping," Maria said as she sat up. Her first thought was that Oswaldo had found them.

"Please, don't be afraid." The voice was kind and gentle.

Maria cautiously poked her head out from behind the bush. "Who's there?" she whispered.

"Please. You must be hungry," the voice said. "Come over to the gate, and I will open it for you."

"This is definitely a dream," Maria said. No one would invite her into his or her home for a meal in the middle of the night.

"Come in," repeated the voice. "I'll explain everything while you eat."

"Who are you?" asked Maria nervously. She could tell it wasn't a woman's voice, but it was high, like a child's.

Victor glanced at his sister. "Who's that?"

"Shhhh."

"I'm so hungry," he whispered.

"Come on." She crawled out from under the bush. "They might know something about where Mama went."

The wooden gate in the wall was about twenty feet down from the bush. The gate swung open.

Maria grabbed her brother's hand and peeked through the gate. The shadows in the garden were dense and dark. "There's no one here."

"Please, you are welcome," the voice said warmly.

Was Oswaldo disguising his voice? wondered Maria. *Was that why the person speaking was hiding?* She shook her head. "If this is a dream, I might as well enjoy it."

Victor pulled on his sister's hand. Together, the two children stepped into the courtyard.

Inside was a well-tended garden with flowers and trees. A small red-tile patio lay in front of the house. Grass bordered the flower beds.

"This is so creepy," she whispered. Maria jumped at the sound of the gate swinging closed. She spun around, ready for anything—but not for what she saw before her.

"It's a monkey!" cried Victor excitedly.

The monkey bowed and introduced herself. "I am Fulang."

"Hi, dream monkey." Maria giggled.

"Come with me and I'll get you something to eat." Fulang turned and led them through the garden.

From the shadows came a rustling of leaves. Maria and Victor leaped back. Then another monkey appeared before them.

"I am Caimito," he said, bowing formally.

Playing along, Maria curtsied. "Pleased to meet you. I am Maria, and this is my brother, Victor."

Victor waved. "*Hola.*"

Maria marveled at the notion of two monkeys talking as they went into the blue-colored house. *This is really a great dream,* she thought.

"Oh, fabulous, look what the monkey dragged in," cracked Chica from the back of the couch.

"A cat that talks!" Maria ran over to Chica and started scratching her behind her ears.

"Finally, someone who knows how to treat a cat," purred Chica. She rolled onto her belly.

The skull laughed, his jaws clacking loudly.

"A candy skull!" marveled Victor. "And it talks!"

"Everyone talks in Casa Azul," explained Fulang.

"Everyone—talks?" said Maria. She watched the portrait of Dr. Eloesser turn in his frame.

"Welcome," said the portrait of Dr. Eloesser and the mother and child in the painting.

The other paintings also welcomed the children.

"It must be the hunger," said Maria. She took her brother's hand again and turned to leave. "Thank you, we've had a nice time—"

But the two monkeys blocked the doorway. "Don't be afraid. This is a magical house," explained Fulang. "We have all been touched with the magic of its owner, Frida."

"Frida? Frida Kahlo?" marveled Maria. "This is Frida's house?"

"*Sí,*" replied Fulang with dignity.

"I just learned about her, and I saw Diego's murals in the Ministry of Public Education."

"Then you know that she is a great painter," Fulang said. She spread her arms. "Like her paintings, which stretch the limits of the real world, so does her home."

"I don't understand," replied Maria.

Fulang led them into the house and explained. "She has suffered so much that her home has become a haven for all. Anyone or anything entering through these walls is touched by her gift."

Maria was amazed. She shook her head. "It seems impossible," she murmured.

"But it's true. And this place can be a haven for you too. You look as if you could use one," added Caimito.

Maria pinched her arm to wake herself. "Ouch!" She shook her arm.

Fulang glanced at Caimito. "There's no need to hurt yourself. We're very real. You're not dreaming."

"Go on, you banana thief," Chica meowed. "There's nothing to be afraid of. Frida will love them. If the painting of the doctor is right, then these children are here to help her."

"They know about El Corazón and El Diablo. The girl was telling the story," clacked the skull.

"And Frida loves children," said Fulang. "Come along, children. We're going to see Frida."

"Maybe it's time to trust a couple of monkeys," muttered Maria.

A warm light shown from under the door of the studio, indicating that Frida was still working. Fulang knocked gently.

"Yes?" responded Frida.

"We have a surprise," said Fulang.

"Wonderful! Come in," called Frida.

"She likes surprises," clattered the skull.

"Shut up, pseudo-bonehead," Chica snapped. "Open the door," added the cat impatiently. She circled in front of the door and then jumped up and put her front paws against it.

Fulang reached up and turned the knob. The door swung open quickly in response to Chica's push.

"What have we here?" exclaimed Frida, setting down her brush. She was much farther along on her self-portrait with the thorn necklace and the hummingbird. Both Caimito and Chica looked so violent in it that Fulang was startled.

Chica examined the painting. "There's a real likeness here."

"There is *not*," snapped Fulang, then she remembered her manners. "Frida, listen to me. These children need food and shelter."

"Children!" cried Frida with delight. She stood and opened her arms in welcome to Maria and Victor.

Fulang was stunned to see that the self-portrait was nearly finished. How long would it be before Frida followed Dorothy?

"Now, don't be rude, Fulang," Frida said pleasantly. "Introduce me to our guests."

"The cat must've got her tongue," purred Chica. "These two turned up on our doorstep."

"I am pleased to meet you." Frida shook both children's hands. "I am Frida."

Maria introduced herself and her brother. They both stared at

Frida's thick, dark eyebrows that connected at the center of her face like a giant black caterpillar perched over her eyes.

Frida examined their disheveled state, the hollow look in their cheeks and eyes. "You must have quite a story to tell, but first you must be hungry." She led them to the kitchen and set out bowls of green chili with goat milk and tortillas for them.

"*Gracias,*" Maria said. She and Victor were starving.

But Victor was enchanted by the house. He kept waving at every object and saying hello. Each time something replied, he collapsed in a fit of giggles.

At the table the pepper shaker in the shape of a rooster said, "Pepper."

"Salt," replied the chicken salt shaker.

"Pepper."

"Salt."

Victor erupted into laughter so hard that the milk in his mouth sprayed the room.

"Victor!" Maria was horrified.

Victor wiped his face with his sleeve and ate quietly.

"Pepper."

"Salt."

Victor tried not to laugh but wasn't successful.

Maria scowled at her brother's bad manners.

Nevertheless, their appetite pleased Frida. Contented, Maria tried to explain their presence. "We've traveled from a village in the north. Our grandmother died, and our priest tried to keep us in the village—"

Frida cut her off, noticing Victor's drooping eyelids. "You both look so exhausted. All this can wait until the morning when you're rested."

"*Gracias,*" replied Maria shyly.

"Let's get you to bed, and we'll talk in the morning." She led them to the guest room. The bed was high and fat like a big loaf of bread, whiter and cleaner than anything Maria had ever seen before. It looked so marvelous and comfortable that she was hesitant to even climb onto it. She didn't want to mess it up.

Victor, on the other hand, immediately dived into the big, fluffy pillows, wrapped himself in the nubby bedspread, and burrowed into the sheets starched and ironed and edged with crocheted lace. Maria was astonished at how many pillows were piled on the bed. Pillows on top of pillows, on top of more pillows—with beautiful embroidery of doves and flowers and sayings. One pillow read *Amor di mi vida.* Love of my life. Another, *Sólo tú.* Only you. Another had the phrase *Amor eterno.* Eternal love. Maria felt so embraced by this extraordinary, outsized love that Frida seemed to have that she finally began to relax for the first time in days. Casa Azul was the most beautiful home they had ever been in. It was much larger than the small one-room adobe house they'd lived in back in their village. But more than its luxury, its magical quality made Maria feel safe. It seemed to vibrate with safety and warmth.

"Sweet dreams," Frida said as she closed the door.

"Maria, tell me a story." Victor yawned sleepily.

Happily, Maria obliged. "As you remember, El Diablo was nearly knocked out on the floor outside the ring, but he quickly recovered. He shook his head to get his senses back. Then slowly he stood and stared with extreme anger at Quetzalcoatl, who circled the ring in triumph. As he watched this Aztec god, he knew that he could not defeat such an amazing and powerful force as the god of life. Quetzalcoatl was all too overwhelming, especially as he drew in the life force from the cheering crowd. If he was to win, there was only one thing for El Diablo to do. He had to do something that no wrestler had ever done in the ring, something that went against the rules and the spirit of wrestling. He reached behind his head and untied the back of his mask. Then slowly, but with evil determination, he slipped the mask off his face."

"No," gasped Victor groggily.

"*Sí.* He pulled off the mask to reveal that he was not just an evil wrestler. Underneath his evil mask lived an even more evil identity. He was the ancient Aztec god of war, Huitzilopochtli, the exact opposite of life. He was . . . death." Maria paused and looked down at Victor. He was already fast asleep.

"This will be the greatest battle in the history of wrestling," she whispered. She kissed the top of his head.

"Sweet dreams," murmured a portrait of Frida's sister that hung on the wall over the bed.

CHAPTER NINETEEN

Hope

Maria tried to sleep. She buried her face in a pillow like an ostrich. She flopped from side to side like a beached whale. She curled into a ball like a caterpillar. But she couldn't fall asleep. Her mind raced over the events of the last few days. Finally she was afraid she would wake Victor, so she quietly climbed out of the bed, planning to sit in a chair and look out the window.

Voices from the other room, however, drew her to the door. She pressed her ear against it and listened. Frida and Fulang were discussing them, wondering where they came from and where their parents were.

A desire to talk and maybe find answers overcame her shyness. Maria opened the door and walked into the living room.

"You should rest," Frida said, seeing her.

"I can't sleep."

"Then let's get you some warm milk." Frida led Maria into the kitchen. "It'll help you sleep." She poured milk into a saucepan and lit the burner on the stove.

"Salt," said the salt shaker.

"Pepper," replied the pepper shaker.

Frida smiled. "I heard you telling your brother the wrestling story. It was wonderful."

"Thank you," said Maria.

"But you know Quetzalcoatl must never defeat Huitzilopochtli, or the other way around."

Maria knit her brow in confusion.

"They must always be in balance. We must have both life and death, peace and war, happiness and anger. Without one the other cannot really exist." Frida poured the warm milk into a mug. "Drink this."

Maria sat at the breakfast table and sipped the milk. "I don't understand. Don't you always want the good to win?"

"In children's stories, of course. But in life we must experience the pain to appreciate the pleasure. Both good and bad must live in a delicate balance."

"Then my story is all wrong," replied Maria. "I was planning to have Quetzalcoatl tear Huitzilopochtli limb from limb so that there would be peace in the world forever."

Frida smiled. "If only it could be so." Frida pulled her shawl tightly around her shoulders and flexed her aching foot. "It just occurred to me that I have been doing the same, but only the opposite."

"What?"

"Lately, the world has seemed a very bad place," explained Frida. "So I've been preparing myself for death."

"You're dying?"

Frida shrugged. "Sometimes it takes the darkest dark of night to finally find the courage to admit the truth." She looked into Maria's eyes. "I've been planning to kill myself."

"No!"

Frida sipped her hot milk and thought for a minute. "Well, I was feeling that the world could only get worse so I might as well leave it."

"But there's so much good. There's so many things to see and experience," protested Maria, her mind flashing to all the things she wanted to do in her life.

"Well, this is true," admitted Frida. "But I've been painting myself into a corner and now either I kill myself or face the paint." She laughed ruefully at her own joke.

Maria didn't quite understand and looked at Frida quizzically.

Frida took her hand and squeezed it. "When I was a young girl not much older than you, Diego told me, 'Art is like ham. It nourishes.' I don't think I quite understood that before. Until I met you."

Maria blushed.

"If I am going to find hope and nourishment, I have to look toward my art, my painting. That's what Diego's been trying to tell me all along, and until I do that he can't be with me." Frida poured more milk into Maria's cup. "Does that taste good?"

"Mmmm."

Maria and Frida sat at the table in silence.

Fulang watched from the doorway. For the first time in days, she had a sense of optimism.

"So why have you ended up in Coyoacán?" asked Frida.

Maria blew into her cup and answered. "We're looking for our mother."

"Do you know where she is?" asked Frida with concern.

"We thought we did." Maria dug the envelope with the address out of her pocket and showed it to Frida.

"Lourdes 27," Frida read aloud. "That's the Cisneros's home. They moved."

"We discovered that today when we found the house," explained Maria, pulling out her mother's handkerchief. "This is the only thing we found in the house . . . my mother's favorite handkerchief." Her shoulders slumped.

Frida took the hanky. "It is beautiful." The handkerchief was embroidered with red and green thread depicting several cacti and a heart. After a moment she said, "Well, I know they've moved north, to Detroit in the United States. Alfredo is an engineer and has gotten a job with Henry Ford. Diego and I have spent a lot of time in Detroit and have many friends. I recommended Alfredo to Mr. Ford, and he moved him up there."

"Oh," said Maria. "Did my mother go with them?"

"Was your mother Ana, their cook?"

"Yes, Ana Ortiz. She left our village last year to work here in the city. She wanted to send for us as soon as she could." Maria looked up at Frida.

"Of course Ana went," replied Frida. "What a wonderful cook she is. And she always talked about her beautiful children. Didn't she write that she was going north?"

Maria shook her head.

"She must have. The letter must have been lost. Ana would never abandon you." Frida looked down at her own cup of milk. "No mother would." She stood. "Well, I'll see what I can do to find your mother. Now, you must go to sleep." She led Maria back to the guest room. "You can stay with us until we find her."

Maria smiled with gratitude, feeling hopeful. "I guess you're right. I'd better get some sleep. Good night." She left Frida in the kitchen and returned to the guest bedroom.

For a moment Casa Azul was quiet except for the chirps and squeaks of the night. Then—

"*Noooooooo!!!!*" screamed Maria long and loud.

Maria fell to her knees before the bed.

"Noooooooo!!!" she sobbed. "It's empty!"

Frida and Fulang dashed into the room.

"It's empty!"

"What's empty?" asked Fulang.

Maria pointed at the bed. The blankets and sheet had been pulled back roughly, and Victor was gone. Curtains fluttered at the open window.

"How? Why?" gasped Frida. She bent over Maria to help her. Fulang leaped through the window to search the courtyard.

"Someone stole the kid," said the portrait of Frida's sister.

"Oswaldo," said Maria as her chest heaved. "It has to be him. He *must* have been the one buying tortillas."

"Tortillas? Who's Oswaldo?" asked Frida with concern.

Maria explained how Oswaldo had tried to kidnap Victor earlier that day and had perhaps followed them to Lourdes.

Fulang returned. "There's no sign of anyone."

Frida stiffened. "Why would this boy want Victor?" she asked.

"I don't know, but his father, Oscar, seemed very interested in my brother," explained Maria between sobs. "He also stole my grandma's brooch."

Frida made eye contact with Fulang. They both held it for a moment.

"This is not good. We have to do something," Frida said, her jaw set.

"I'm so tired of standing," said the portrait to no one in particular, and no one answered her. Everyone had already left the room.

CHAPTER TWENTY

Help from Diego

It was like Frida had emerged from a long and deep sleep.

"Fulang, go find Diego," she ordered. Even though they were now divorced, Frida wouldn't consider doing anything without getting Diego's help, and Diego wouldn't without Frida. *Nothing has really changed,* thought Frida. *Diego will come and help. We are still hopelessly linked to each other.*

Fulang dashed out the window.

"Wait!" shouted Frida after her. Fulang returned.

"Is there any place your brother might go?" she asked Maria.

"The plaza in the center of the city."

"Good," said Frida. Then she turned to Fulang. "Take Diego to the plaza in the center of the city. We'll meet him there in an hour."

Suddenly Frida was her old self. The great sadness that had blanketed her was gone.

"I must sit for a minute." Frida sat on the couch. "My leg is hurting today. There will be rain soon."

"How do you know?" asked Maria.

"Whenever the barometer drops, the leg I shattered in my accident aches. It is doing it now." She rubbed her leg and pointed to a cane by the door. "Could you bring me that?"

Maria got the cane and handed it to her.

Frida stood and leaned on it. "Let's go."

On the trolley to town, Frida took Maria's hand. "We'll send Alfredo a telegram first and then we'll meet Diego."

It was already early morning. The darkness was beginning to disappear in the dawn light. In the grand plaza, children were playing the blind game, taking turns walking through the crowds with their eyes shut, one leading, the other being led.

"*¿Qué quiere usted?*
Mata rile rile rile.

Yo quiero una niña.
Mata rile rile ron.

Escoja usted.
Mata rile rile rile.

Escojo a Juan.
Mata rile rile ron."

Que oficio le pondremos?
Mata rile rile rile.

"What do you want?
Mata rile rile rile.

I want a girl.
Mata rile rile ron.

Choose who you would like.
Mata rile rile rile.

I pick Juan.
Mata rile rile ron.

What job should we give him?
Mata rile rile rile."

Children danced around, singing and laughing.

Maria almost cried. "Victor loved the blind game."

"Don't worry, we'll find him," said Frida grimly. "Now, where did you first meet this boy?"

"By the fountain where Viejo Ojoton sings." Maria pointed.

The old man was playing his guitar on the same bench that Maria and Victor had been sitting on just two days before. To Maria, that seemed ages ago.

"There's Diego! Diego!" Frida shouted and waved.

With Fulang perched on his shoulder, Diego hurried over the Frida. His massive bulk spread the crowd like a steamship in the ocean. "*Mi vida,* my life!"

"Oh, Diego! It is terrible." Frida turned to Maria. "This girl has lost her brother and we must help her."

Diego nodded. He did not question Frida's quest. "Of course. Where?"

Maria, awed by being in the presence of such a famous person, explained what had happened.

"Fulang," said Diego.

Fulang stood at attention, awaiting his direction. Though she could not speak, she could still understand.

"Go out and talk to the monkeys in the city. We must find this boy now!"

Fulang dashed away through the crowd.

They returned to Casa Azul dejected. Maria thought she might be sick. The urgency in Diego's voice brought home once again the reality of the danger that Victor was in and how little they knew. They had searched all day for Victor and for Oswaldo's secret cave, but they had not found either. Maria had tried to remember exactly how they had gotten to the cave from the plaza, but the city was like a maze to her. She couldn't even find the window where she had seen the toy maker.

Still, when it became clear that they were not going to find Victor by randomly searching the streets of the city, Maria did not want to stop. Frida and Diego convinced her that they must return home to find out if there was any news from Fulang. Reluctantly, Maria agreed.

"You must eat," Frida said as she set a plate of tamales in front of Maria.

"I'm not hungry." Maria tucked a strand of hair behind her ear because it had been tickling her neck and looked away. "Where's Fulang?"

"She'll be here soon," answered Frida.

Diego pulled the plate in front of himself and dug in. "These are good, Frida. I miss your cooking."

"Then why'd you leave me?" Frida plopped into a chair at the table.

"I couldn't help it," mumbled Diego with his mouth full. "You were suffocating with me."

Frida picked up a knife and gestured violently with it. "I'm not suffocating anymore!"

Diego put up his hands. "Frida, put down the knife. We need to worry about this poor girl and her kidnapped brother."

Frida dropped the knife on the table. "You're right," she said with resignation.

Crash! A flowerpot on the windowsill hit the floor and shattered.

"Oops! Sorry about that," said Caimito as he skittered, off balance, through the window.

"Caimito! Where's Fulang?" said Diego.

"Never mind that. Do you have any news?" asked Frida.

"Victor is breaking into the Federica Diamond Exchange," replied Caimito. "Hurry! Fulang is already on her way there." He went back out the window and scurried across the garden. Then he stopped, realizing that humans could not follow him this way. "Hurry!" he called, waiting for them to come through the doorway.

CHAPTER TWENTY-ONE

Monkey Shines

As Fulang entered the alley, she spotted Victor twenty feet up, hanging from the side of the Federica Diamond Exchange and Oswaldo pacing below. She could see that Victor was too frightened to move either up to the window or back down.

"Climb!" Oswaldo shouted.

Without thinking, she effortlessly scaled the building. She tried to calm Victor, but all she could do was screech and pat him.

"My fingers hurt," he told her. It was clear he would not be able to hold on much longer.

Alarmed, Fulang tried to coach the boy in how to climb back down by miming each step, but Victor was too frightened to move.

Quickly Fulang descended to the alley in search of something or someone to help. The alley was now empty. Oswaldo had disappeared as the sounds of sirens came closer and closer. The police would be there any minute. Unfortunately, Fulang didn't think Victor could hold on for even that one minute. She searched around the alley for something, anything to save this boy. She ran to one end of the alley. Nothing. She ran to the other end. Still nothing. Frantically, she climbed onto an empty packing crate, thinking that it might break Victor's fall. Then she saw the answer.

A rope!

The crate had a rope loosely tied around it. Fulang immediately untangled it and scaled the wall once more with the rope between her teeth. In one fluid movement she tied the rope around Victor's waist.

Her great idea began to sink, however, when she realized she wouldn't be able to hold Victor with the rope. Even though he was only eight years old, he was still six times her weight.

There must a solution, Fulang thought. She glanced up and noticed that there were shutters on the window above them. The shutter on the right had a big iron latch that was used to lock this shutter to the one on the left. If she tied the rope to it, perhaps it would hold. In one swift leap the monkey flew up to the shutter and tied a nice tight knot around the big iron latch.

"I can't hold on any longer!" cried Victor. His fingers slipped from the stone crevice. He fell a couple of feet, but then the rope drew taut and stopped his fall. Victor held on to the rope and swung silently below the window, too frightened to scream.

"There he is!" came a shout. Frida led Diego, Maria, and Caimito down the alley.

Fulang scurried down the wall to greet Frida who looked exhausted.

The five of them stood helplessly below the boy dangling twenty feet up in the air.

"Don't worry, Victor. We'll get you," called Maria.

"I'm scared," cried Victor.

Suddenly, there was a crack. The iron bracket was beginning to pull away from the shutter.

"Do something!" screamed Maria. "He's going to fall!"

Leaning on her cane, Frida hobbled down the alley looking for anything that might help, but Fulang had already found the only thing of use.

Maria started to climb up the stone wall, but she quickly fell back. Her fingers and toes were too big to fit into the crevices like Victor's.

CRAAAAAACK!

The iron bracket broke away a little more.

"Stand back," commanded Diego. He waved his arms for everyone to step away from the wall.

CRAAAAAAACK!

The bracket broke free. Victor dropped like a rock, straight down. His arms flailed out. He kicked his legs spasmodically in an attempt to somehow stop himself. But he could not.

Victor fell helplessly toward the ground.

"Victor!" Maria screamed.

Diego stepped up to the wall below Victor and caught the boy in his massive arms. He staggered under the impact but kept his balance. The bracket just passed his head and slammed into the ground. Then he raised Victor for everyone to see. "He's safe!"

Maria ran over to the two as Diego set Victor down.

"Don't scare me like that," she told her brother as she hugged him tightly. "I don't think I could live if I lost you." They both cried.

"Hold it right there!" shouted a policeman, interrupting the reunion. "Everyone up against the wall!" He had out his gun.

A moment later five other policemen were in the alley with their guns pointed at the group.

"We've caught them red-handed!" shouted the policeman to the other officers.

Diego held out his arms with his hands open. "Please, we're not thieves."

"Don't argue with me!" shouted the first policeman. "Up against the wall!"

They all put their hands against the wall.

Another policeman did a double take as he got closer. "Diego? Diego Rivera?" He rushed down the alley and grabbed the first policeman's arm. "Alejandro, this is Diego Rivera."

The first policeman suddenly realized his mistake. "Oh, Diego, I am so sorry."

"*Esta bien, no te preocupes.* It is nothing," said Diego, stepping away from the wall. "And this is Frida." He waved his hand toward his former wife.

Frida stepped forward. "I am so grateful that you have arrived."

"What is going on here?" a sergeant barked when he entered the alley.

"An attempt to rob the diamond exchange was thwarted by these brave children," explained Diego, lying just a little. He pointed to Maria and Victor, standing speechless behind him. "They are heroes of Mexico!"

The policemen holstered their weapons.

Diego stepped out of the way. "These two small friends of ours, Victor and Maria . . . uh . . ."

"Ortiz," added Maria.

"Yes, well, Victor and Maria Ortiz alerted Frida and myself to this plan to break into the Federica Diamond Exchange," explained Diego.

"Right up there!" pointed Victor, gaining courage from Diego. "That third-floor window."

The policemen looked up.

"That's pretty high up," said one officer skeptically.

"That's why the thieves wanted me to climb up," answered Victor, rather enjoying being the center of attention.

"The boy's sister called us," interjected Diego. "And Frida and I came right away, but young Victor here had already scared away the thieves."

"Not too far away!" The noise from a scuffle echoed down the alleyway as a policeman dragged Oswaldo back to the scene of the attempted crime. "I found this little rodent running away, about a block from here," explained the officer.

"I didn't do anything," cried Oswaldo. "I was going home to my sick mother."

The policeman threw Oswaldo to the ground. "Don't lie to me, you sewer rat. I've seen you before. You're hooked up with that thief they call Oscar."

"No!" shrieked Oswaldo.

"You're going to the work farm," said the policeman. He started to drag the boy away.

"Wait!" shouted Oswaldo. He broke free of the police officer and ran to Maria. He dug into his pocket and pulled out the brooch.

"My brooch!"

"I didn't give it to Oscar. I was going to because he wanted me to steal it from you, but I didn't." He handed the brooch to Maria. "I would never hurt you."

Maria looked down at the brooch. Then impulsively she kissed Oswaldo. She turned to Diego and Frida. "We can't let them take him. He only needs someone to help him be good."

Frida took Maria's hand. "There's not much we can do."

"Please! He didn't mean it. He was just scared of that awful man."

"Doesn't matter," replied the sergeant. "He's a thief, and we've been looking for him for a while."

"But he wants to be good," pressed Maria. "Just give him a chance."

The sergeant looked at the officer who held Oswaldo. "Okay," he said, speaking to Oswaldo. "Tell us where to find Oscar, and we'll get you in the orphanage instead of the work farm."

Oswaldo nodded. Quietly he said, "He's in Cutter's Alley. The old door that's off its hinges leads to a cave underground. He's in there."

CHAPTER TWENTY-TWO

A New Happiness

In the middle of the night, Maria finally knew what the outcome to the wrestling championship of the world was to be. She couldn't wait to tell Victor. It was early, and his eyes were half shut, but soon they widened.

"As I was telling you before, El Corazón had transformed himself into a stone statue of the Aztec god of life, Quetzalcoatl," she said, "while El Diablo had become a stone statue of Huitzilopochtli, the Aztec god of war. Now, even though they were made of stone, they were still gods and able to move. In fact, the stone gave them even greater strength. While the crowd went wild, the two gods squared off in the ring and circled each other. With each move that one would perform, the other would do an equally effective counter-move. This meant that neither of these two gods would ever get the upper hand over the other. Instead, they wound up in eternal combat with each other, the wrestling match going on and on forever. The crowds would come and go, watching some of the match for a while and then moving on."

"There's no winner?" asked Victor, disappointed.

"No winner," explained Maria. "Instead, the two gods must battle each other through eternity, always at a standstill. If one ever wins, the balance between good and evil in the world would end and so would the world."

"But what if good wins, isn't that better?" pressed Victor.

"It seems as if it would make sense that if good triumphs, the world would be a better place," said Maria. "But you must remember. Without evil there is no good. The two must balance each other. It is the way of the world. So neither can win." Maria's thoughts turned to Oswaldo.

"I don't think I understand this," replied Victor.

"You will," Maria said.

Knock! Knock!

"Are you two awake?" called Frida.

"Please, come in," said Maria.

"I have news!" She held out the telegraph. "Let's open it together." Maria tore open the envelope and the three of them read it.

```
Children STOP Weeping with joy STOP
Letter lost STOP Coming to get you
STOP Till next week STOP Love Mama
```

CHAPTER TWENTY-THREE

A New Portrait

That night, long after everyone had gone to bed after spending the day preparing for Ana Ortiz's arrival, Frida padded through the house and entered her studio.

Fulang, who slept lightly, awoke when Frida opened the door. Silently, she crept into the studio to watch over Frida as she worked.

Frida gazed for a few minutes at her *Self-Portrait with Thorn Necklace and Hummingbird.*

A sick feeling overcame Fulang at the sight of this painting. She wanted to leave, but her loyalty to Frida was too strong.

Frida sat, looking at her image. Once Frida picked up her brush, Fulang settled in a corner of the studio where she could not see the painting. She sat and watched Frida work until eventually she fell asleep.

Frida painted through the night, filling in the dark background and defining the foreground with herself, Caimito, and Chica. She worked feverishly, painting an image in and painting it out and repainting it. Thick layers of paint built up on the canvas, making it as dense as the tropical forest in the background. Frida's eyebrows became one long single brow that cut across her forehead, almost like a crown. Caimito's and Chica's faces became more distinct and full of expression. The blood on Frida's neck grew a darker crimson. Dawn broke through the gauze curtains of the room. In the morning light Frida looked at the painting and decided it was done.

"Wake up, monkey," she called to Fulang.

Fulang yawned and stretched. She had forgotten that she had fallen asleep in Frida's studio and so for a moment was disoriented. Groggily she came over to where Frida was painting. She had forgotten that Frida was working on the painting that gave her such sorrow. She was simply pleased that Frida seemed to have moved on from the depression of the last few days.

That changed, however, when she glanced up at the canvas on the easel. Fulang thought she was going to faint.

"You like?" asked Frida playfully.

"Y—y—yes!" stammered Fulang.

On the easel was the portrait of Frida, Caimito, and Chica; but it had changed dramatically. On Frida's right shoulder, Caimito no longer looked menacing. In fact, he seemed more playful than dangerous to Fulang. His hand wasn't pulling at the thorn necklace. Though a thorn still broke the skin on Frida's neck, it was unclear whether Caimito had put it there or was trying to alleviate the pain by pulling it. On Frida's left shoulder, Chica had dropped the hummingbird. Though the bird was still dead, it merely hung from the thorn necklace, while Chica looked down at it without expression.

"You've changed it," Fulang finally said.

Frida put down her brush. "I finally decided to take my own

advice. The gods demanded it. Like the battle between Quetzalcoatl and Huitzilopochtli, neither death nor life can triumph. There always must be a balance between joy and sorrow. It can never be all or nothing. It is always somewhere in between."

Frida picked up the canvas and carried it awkwardly into the living room. She replaced the portrait of Dr. Eloesser with it. She moved stiffly as if all her joints needed to be oiled.

"We didn't need Dr. Eloesser after all," Chica said to Fulang.

"Well, not the living one at least," said Fulang. "The portrait helped us."

"This will be the painting I display at my Cinco de Mayo fiesta," said Frida.

Fulang felt as if the celebration had already begun. Impulsively she leaped into the garden and found Caimito napping in a tree. She quickly climbed the tree and gave Caimito a peck on the cheek, startling the monkey awake.

Frida Kahlo's Life and Art

Frida Kahlo's life was a long struggle between extreme physical suffering and an extraordinary hunger for life. She overcame her physical limitations and pain through sheer will to become one of Mexico's greatest artists.

Much like the way she painted and lived her life, Frida fabricated her birth date so that it corresponded with how she perceived herself. During her life she claimed that she was born on July 7, 1910, the same year as the beginning of the Mexican Revolution. To her the fact that she was actually born on July 6, 1907, had no relevance. What mattered was how she felt in her heart. She identified with the incredible optimism and hope that the revolution brought to many Mexicans despite the suffering that war also brings. Like the revolution, Frida was full of hope in spite of pain.

At age six, Frida contracted polio. Although she recovered, her right leg never fully developed and always remained thinner than her left. But this setback did not deter her. By the time she entered high school at the prestigious National Prepatory School, she was a tomboy full of mischief. Despite being one of only thirty-five girls among two thousand boys, Frida quickly became the ringleader of a rebellious and intellectually ambitious group called the *Cachuchas*. They were known to play pranks on teachers at the school. In 1922, while Diego Rivera was completing his mural in the Bolívar Amphitheater at the school, Frida became infatuated with him. Legend has it that at the time she declared to her friends: "My ambition is to have a child with Diego Rivera. And I'm going to tell him someday." Nothing came of this infatuation at the time, but she did play a few pranks on Diego, such as stealing his lunch, while he was working. So although they had not yet met, he was aware of her.

The accident that would affect the rest of her life occurred three years later, on September 17, 1925. She and a friend spent the day wandering the colorful street stalls that were set up for the Mexican National Day celebration. As evening approached, they boarded a passing bus to return to Coyoacán, the suburb of Mexico City where she lived. As the driver rushed through the city, he tried to pass in front of a turning trolley. The heavy trolley broadsided the bus. The accident left Frida Kahlo with a broken spinal column, a broken collarbone, broken ribs, a broken pelvis, and eleven fractures in her right leg. In addition, her right foot was dislocated and crushed, and her left shoulder was out of joint. For a month Frida was forced to stay flat on her back, encased in a plaster cast and enclosed in a boxlike structure. During her convalescence from the accident she began painting because she was bored. This became her lifelong profession.

To her doctor's surprise, Frida regained her ability to walk. However, for the rest of her life she lived in tremendous pain and suffered debilitating fatigue. She was sometimes hospitalized for long periods of time or bedridden for months, and thirty-five operations were performed over the last twenty-nine years of her life. To manage the pain, she turned to alcohol, drugs, and cigarettes, none of which helped much.

It was painting that sustained her and provided entrée into the artistic scene of Mexico, where she met Diego Rivera again. She took four little paintings to Diego, who was painting on scaffolds at the Ministry of Public Education. Diego liked her work and encouraged her. Soon they became involved and were married on August 21, 1929. Over the next eleven years, their marriage was a tumultuous relationship that took them to Detroit, New York, and France, among other places. Though deeply in love, both had affairs with other people; and they fought ferociously. Their marriage has been called the union between an elephant and a dove, because Diego was huge and very fat, and Frida was small (a little more than five feet) and slender.

Despite Diego's affairs with other women (one with Frida's sister), he supported Frida's art completely and was a dogged promoter of her work. He recommended that she begin wearing traditional Mexican clothing, which consisted of long, colorful dresses and exotic jewelry. These garments, along with Frida's thick, connecting eyebrows, became the trademark of her self-portraits. Frida in turn was Diego's most trusted critic and the love of his life.

What carried Frida through her constant pain was her indomitable spirit. She was outgoing and witty. She liked to sprinkle her conversation with vivid expletives. She loved to drink tequila and sing off-color songs to guests at the crazy parties she hosted. Men were fascinated by her, and because of this Frida had numerous, scandalous affairs. Frida was a bisexual and also had affairs with many women.

In 1937 she had an affair with the Communist leader Leon Trotsky. Both Frida and Diego were committed communists who participated in numerous protests. This was why Trotsky had come to stay at her home, along with his wife. Frida was later arrested for his murder but was released. Diego was also under suspicion. Several years after Trotsky's death, Diego and Frida enjoyed telling people that they invited him to Mexico just to get him killed, but no one knows if they were telling the truth or not. They were fantastic storytellers.

All over the world people loved Frida. In 1938, when she went to France, she became the darling of the French surrealist movement. Pablo Picasso became so enamored of her that he made her a pair of earrings. During her visit, she even appeared on the cover of the French magazine *Vogue*. Her work was included in shows in the United States and in Mexico.

In 1940 Frida and Diego divorced but remarried within a year. It was during the year of the divorce, however, that Frida was able to step out from behind Diego's shadow and find herself as an artist. Frida painted the world as she experienced it, not as it was. Her canvases recorded her emotional reality, which did not always correspond to physical reality. Using jarring colors and odd spatial relationships, she painted the anger and hurt over her stormy marriage, the painful miscarriages, and the physical suffering she underwent because of the accident. Many of her pictures include startling symbolic images and elements from Mexican history.

Even after they remarried, Frida continued living at Casa Azul, the home in which she was born; Diego would visit and occasionally spend the night. After the divorce Frida tried to be independent of Diego. Perhaps as a result, the five years after their remarriage were the most serene of their married life.

In 1943, at Diego's suggestion, Frida began teaching at the Ministry of Public Education's experimental new School for Painting and Sculpture. Shortly after starting to teach, Frida's health made it impossible for her to travel to the school, so her students came to Casa Azul. Despite her failing health, Frida continued to paint. These years were her most productive.

With Frida's health getting worse, by 1950 her doctor thought a bone graft might decrease her pain. This operation proved disastrous. The implanted bone caused a severe infection, and Frida spent the next nine months in the hospital.

Frida only had one exhibition in Mexico, and it was in the spring of 1953. Her health was very bad by this time. She had recently had her right leg amputated below the knee because of the gangrenous condition of her foot. In her diary she wrote the poignant phrase, *"Pies para qué los quiero, si tengo alas pa' volar?"* ("Feet—why do I need them if I have wings to fly?")

Her doctors advised that she not attend her solo exhibition. Minutes after guests were allowed into the gallery, sirens were heard outside. The crowd went crazy when they saw an ambulance accompanied by a motorcycle escort. Frida Kahlo had arrived. She was placed in the middle of the gallery in her bed, Frida told jokes, entertained the crowd, sang, and drank the whole evening. The exhibition was an amazing success.

Over the next few months, however, Frida's health deteriorated quickly. On July 13, 1954, Frida died. On her death certificate her doctor wrote that the cause of death was a pulmonary embolism. Her death might have been the result of an accidental drug overdose or suicide, but no autopsy was performed. Her last words in her diary read, "*Espero alegre la salida—y espero no volver jamás.*" In English that means, "I hope this exit is joyful—and I hope never to return."

A Timeline of Kahlo's Life

1907   On July 6, Magdalena Carmen Frida Kahlo Calderón is born in Coyoacán, Mexico, the third of Matilde Calderón and Guillermo Kahlo's four daughters.

1910   The Mexican Revolution begins. Later in life Kahlo claimed 1910 was the year of her birth.

1913   Frida suffers an attack of polio, permanently affecting the use of her right leg.

1922   Fifteen-year-old Frida enters the National Prepatory School, where she plays pranks on Diego Rivera, who is painting his mural Creation at the school. Though she does not actually meet Rivera, her jokes make an impression on him. She is one of thirty-five girls in a student body of two thousand.

1925   On September 17, Frida nearly dies in a trolley accident. Her spinal column is broken in three places. Her collarbone is broken, and also her third and fourth ribs. Her right leg has eleven fractures, and her right foot is dislocated and crushed. Her left shoulder is out of joint and her pelvis is broken in three places. The steel handrail of the trolley goes straight through her abdomen. She will never fully recover from these injuries.

1926   Frida begins to paint while convalescing at home.

1929   On August 21, Frida marries Rivera. She is twenty-two (nineteen, to those who think she was born in 1910) and he is forty-three.

1931   In San Francisco, Frida meets Dr. Leo Eloesser, who becomes her physician for the rest of her life.

1934   Frida and Diego live in adjoining houses with a bridge between them. Frida has three operations, one to have her appendix removed, one for an abortion, and one because of foot problems.

1935   Frida and Diego separate. Frida moves to an apartment in Mexico City. In July she travels to New York. When she returns, the couple reconcile. She has a foot operation. Her foot takes six months to heal.

1936   Frida experiences intense back pain and has another foot operation.

1937   On January 9, Leon Trotsky and his wife, Natalia Sedova, arrive in Mexico and stay at Casa Azul. (Trotsky was one of the founders of the Soviet Union but had to flee his country when he came under disfavor with the Soviet leadership.) Like Trotsky, Frida and Diego are ardent communists.

1938   French surreallist André Breton visits Mexico and meets Frida. American collector and actor Edward G. Robinson purchases four works, her first significant sale.

From October 25 to November 14, Frida has her first solo exhibition in New York, at the Julian Levy Gallery.

1939   Frida travels to Paris for Mexique, an exhibition curated by André Breton that included her paintings. The Louvre purchases her self-portrait *The Frame*.

Frida returns in April, when Diego begins divorce proceedings against her. The divorce is finalized in November.

1940   In January *The Two Fridas* and *The Wounded Table* are exhibited in the International Surrealism Exhibition organized by the Gallery of Mexican Art. Her *Self-Portrait with Thorn Necklace and Hummingbird* is sold to photographer Nicolas Munay, who had previously purchased her work.

Frida goes to San Francisco for medical treatment by Dr. Eloesser. She shows her work in the San Francisco Golden Gate International Exhibition. *The Two Fridas* is shown in New York at the Museum of Modern Art's exhibition Twenty Centuries of Mexican Art.

On December 8 Frida remarries Diego in San Francisco.

1942   Frida's *Self-Portrait with Braid* is included in the exhibition Twentieth-Century Portraits at the Museum of Modern Art.

1943   One of her paintings is exhibited at the Benjamin Franklin Library in Mexico City in the group show, A Century of Portrait in

Mexico (1830-1942). Her work is also exhibited in Philadelphia, Pennsylvania, and at the Guggenheim Museum in New York.

Frida begins teaching at the Ministry of Public Education's School of Painting and Sculpture, La Esmeralda.

1946   Frida goes to New York for surgery on her spine. She paints *The Wounded Deer* and *Tree of Hope, Stand Fast.*

1947   Her Self-Portrait as a Tehuana is exhibited at the National Institute of Fine Arts, Mexico City.

1949   Frida writes the essay "Portrait of Diego" and paints *Diego and I* and *The Love Embrace of the Universe, the Earth (Mexico), Me, Diego, and Mr. Xólotl,* which is exhibited at the Salon de la Plástica Mexicana in Mexico City.

1950   Frida is hospitalized for nine months because of recurring spinal problems.

1953   From April 13 to 27, Frida's only individual exhibition in Mexico is held at the Galería de Arte Contemporáneo in Mexico City.

In July her leg is amputated below the knee because of gangrene.

1954   Frida is hospitalized in April and May. On July 2, convalescing from bronchial pneumonia, she takes part in a demonstration protesting United States intervention in Guatemala. On the night of July 13, she dies. Her doctor determines she died of pulmonary embolism, but rumors persist that her death was a suicide.

FOR MORE INFORMATION

Readers can learn more about Frida Kahlo's life from:

Frida: A Biography of Frida Kahlo, by Hayden Herrera (New York: Perrenial, 2002).

Frida Kahlo: The Brush of Anguish, by Martha Zamora (San Francisco: Chronicle Books, 1990).

Frida Kahlo: The Paintings, by Hayden Herrera (New York: Perrenial, 2002).

Frida's Fiestas: Recipes and Reminiscences of Life with Frida Kahlo, by Marie Pierre Colle and Guadalupe Rivera (New York: Clarkson Potter, 1994).

The Diary of Frida Kahlo: An Intimate Self-Portrait, by Carlos Fuentes (New York: Harry N. Abrams, 1998).

Look for the teacher's guide to *Casa Azul* at www.wgpub.com.

WHERE TO SEE THE WORK OF FRIDA KAHLO:
MUSEUMS AND WEBSITES

Albright-Knox Art Gallery
1285 Elmwood Avenue
Buffalo, New York 14222-1096
Telephone 716.882.8700
Fax 716.882.1958
www.albrightknox.org

National Museum of Women in the Arts
1250 New York Avenue, N.W.
Washington, DC 20005-3970
202-783-5000, 1-800-222-7270
www.nmwa.org

ArtNet
www.artnet.com

Artchive
www.artchive.com

Phoenix Art Museum
1625 N. Central Ave.
Phoenix , AZ 85004
(602) 257-1222
www.phxart.org

Smoking Mirror:
An Encounter with Paul Gauguin
by Douglas Rees

The White Wolf killed his best friend. Now Joe Sloan seeks revenge. As he navigates the unknown territory of 1891 Tahiti and its people, he finds an unlikely ally in the French artist Paul Gauguin.

Hardcover ISBN: 0-8230-4863-2   Price: $15.95

The Wedding:
An Encounter with Jan van Eyck
by E. M. Rees

In fifteenth-century Belgium, young Giovanna Cenami resists an arranged marriage in favor of true love. Who wouldn't choose a handsome and valiant youth over a seemingly dull merchant ten years her senior? Or is there more than meets the eye?

Hardcover ISBN: 0-8230-0407-4   Price: $15.95